W9-BXH-414

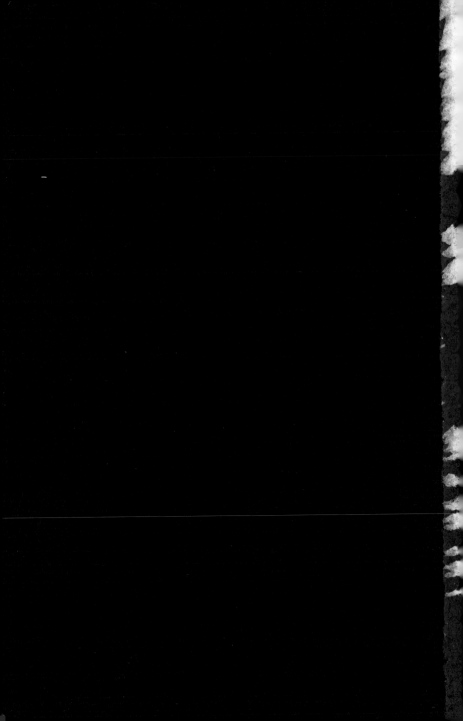

Also by Deborah Ellis

Looking for X
The Breadwinner
Parvana's Journey
Mud City
A Company of Fools
The Heaven Shop
Three Wishes: Palestinian and Israeli Children Speak
Our Stories, Our Songs: African Children Talk About AIDS
I Am a Taxi
Jackal in the Garden: An Encounter with Bihzad Jakeman

SACRED
LEAF

The

Cocalero ✳ ✳ ✳ ✳ ✳ ✳ ✳ ✳

Novels

SACRED
LEAF

✳ ✳ ✳ ✳ ✳ ✳ ✳ ✳ ✳ ✳ ✳

Deborah Ellis

Groundwood Books
House of Anansi Press
Toronto   Berkeley

Groundwood Books / House of Anansi Press
110 Spadina Avenue, Suite 801, Toronto, Ontario M5V 2K4
Distributed in the USA by Publishers Group West
1700 Fourth Street, Berkeley, CA 94710

We acknowledge for their financial support of our publishing program the
Canada Council for the Arts, the Government of Canada through the
Book Publishing Industry Development Program (BPIDP) and the
Ontario Arts Council.

ONTARIO ARTS COUNCIL
CONSEIL DES ARTS DE L'ONTARIO

Library and Archives Canada Cataloguing in Publication
Ellis, Deborah
Sacred Leaf / by Deborah Ellis
(The cocalero novels)
ISBN-13: 978-0-88899-751-7 (bound).—
ISBN-10: 0-88899-751-5 (bound).—
ISBN-13: 978-0-88899-808-8 (pbk.) —
ISBN-10: 0-88899-808-2 (pbk.)
1. Coca industry — Bolivia — Juvenile fiction. 2. Bolivia — Juvenile
fiction. I. Title. II. Series: Ellis, Deborah, Cocalero novels.
PS8559.L5494S23 2007   jC813'.54   C2007-902596-X

Printed and bound in Canada

To those who take their liberation
into their own hands.

The Story So Far

Bolivia, 2000

Twelve-year-old Diego Juárez has spent the past four years living in the women's prison in Cochabamba, Bolivia, where he shares a cell with his mother and his little sister, across the square from his father in the men's prison. He is allowed to come and go, and earns money as a taxi, running errands for other prisoners.

One evening, his daydreaming allows his sister to wander off on her own — something that is not allowed — and his misdeed is made worse when he ruins another prisoner's pot of soup. All of this leaves his mother with a big debt and heavy fines — money she can't pay.

Diego is desperate to earn money and redeem himself, so he and his best friend, Mando, get themselves hired as pit boys, stomping coca leaves into paste. Coca is a sacred plant to the native people of Bolivia, who chew it and brew it as a tea for medicine, and to help them live at high altitudes. But when it is mixed with chemicals and turned into a paste, it becomes the raw ingredient for cocaine, an illegal drug.

Diego and Mando are taken into the jungle by Smith, a mysterious gringo, to work as virtual slaves. But their attempts to receive justice result in Mando's death and Diego's frantic escape through the jungle, with the murderous Smith right on his heels.

Finally, alone, scared and hungry, Diego stumbles upon the small farm belonging to the Ricardo family...

"People lost their fear of bullets."
                                    −Oscar Olivera

CHAPTER ONE

The guinea pigs were loose.

Diego didn't notice at first. The light in the little hut was dim, and it took a moment for his eyes to adjust when he walked in with an armload of firewood. The first hint that all was not right was a sudden movement, a flicker of something at the corner of his eye.

He put the wood down on the drying rack and looked around. Nothing. Just the simple stools, the pallet beds in the corners, the small table and shelves.

Diego had only been living with the Ricardo family for a week, but already their hut felt like home. That was partly because of the way the family – except for Bonita – had welcomed him.

Mostly it was because his old home had been just like this. It was a long time ago, but he still remembered.

"I'm seeing things," he said to Santo. Little Santo giggled, which was his usual two-year-old response to everything, and added his own small stick to the woodpile.

Then Diego saw it again — something darting out from one dark corner to another. After that, it was as if all the guinea pigs had permission to show themselves.

It's only Diego, they seemed to tell each other with their grunts and squeals. He doesn't know much about us. He's too slow. He'll never catch us.

The message spread from one furry creature to another. They dashed and ran and slipped right by Diego, who knew he'd be in big trouble with Bonita if he didn't get them rounded back up. The guinea pigs, an important part of the family's food supply, weren't really his job, but she was always looking for a reason to criticize.

"Close the door," he said to Santo. "In here we have a chance. Out there they have all of Bolivia to run in and hide."

Santo shut the door of the hut, but he was too short to reach the latch. Diego had to do it for him.

When Diego first arrived at the farm, he was too weak to do much farm work, but at least he could look after the little boy. They had become good friends in a short while. Diego had had plenty of experience with Corina, his own little sister.

"First we'd better see if the pen is broken," Diego said. "Otherwise they'll run right out again when we put them back."

Diego bent down to look under the stove where the guinea pigs were kept in a little pen. One of the clay walls had collapsed in the middle.

"It's also pretty dirty under here," he said. "Santo, get me the broom."

The Ricardo family used a broom made from cornstalks tied together. Santo carried it over to the stove, looking very proud of himself since the broom was much taller than he was. Diego was able to get some of the mess out, but not all.

"We need a better system," he said. But first they had to get the guinea pigs back into the old pen.

He took some sticks from the woodpile, bound them together with strips of vine that were drying on a peg to use as string and blocked up the hole in the wall of the pen.

The family had a dozen guinea pigs. They weren't used to being hunted or handled, and they didn't realize that Diego just wanted to put them back where they would be comfortable. Fortunately they didn't climb or jump, and once Diego had herded them into a corner, they were fairly easy to grab.

Santo didn't help much. He was pretending to be a jaguar, leaping and growling.

Ten caught. Diego put his finger to his lips and the two boys went silent, listening for scurrying or squeaking. It was squeaking that gave number eleven away, in a corner of one of the beds.

"Eleven!" Diego triumphantly dumped the stray back in the pen. He tried to listen again, but Santo was too busy growling, and there was also a lot of squealing going on in the pen.

"Number twelve will have to wait," he said. He held out his hand, and Santo cheerfully took it. They left the hut, being careful to latch the door.

The rest of the Ricardo family were all off in

Deborah Ellis

different directions. Mrs. Ricardo was in the forest looking for wild herbs and root vegetables to dig up for a stew. Bonita, who was twelve like Diego, was at the village school with six-year-old Martino, who had just started going to school, a forty-five-minute walk away. Mr. Ricardo was helping a neighbor repair the thatch on his roof.

Diego stood outside the house perched on the side of a hill that looked out over more trees and valleys and hills, everything green and growing.

He pretended, just for a moment, that this was his farm. The neat gardens of potatoes, beans and onions, the few rows of hardy corn, the thick green of the coca bushes beyond that. Mrs. Ricardo liked things to be neat, just like his mother. Large stones outlined a footpath to the door. Also like his mother, Mrs. Ricardo kept flowers by the door. Diego's mother's flowers had been red. These were orange.

Other than that it was the same, right down to the well-scrubbed step by the door.

"Mama's in the forest gathering herbs and roots," he said. "Papa's taking coca to the market. And Corina…" Out of habit, he was going to say, "Corina's been stolen by monkeys," or something like that, because she was always so annoying. But he stopped himself. He and his mother and four-year-old Corina had lived together in a small prison cell back in Cochabamba, and that would make anybody annoying. Out here, though, she'd be too busy helping out and running around to be a bother.

Santo was looking at him and giggling, since it was clear that Diego was talking to himself.

"Santo," said Diego, "let's make those guinea pigs a new home."

A plan was forming in Diego's mind. He saw his mind as a sort of notebook, where he could make notes and do calculations. He began to see what the new pen could look like.

"We need to be able to pull the pen out for easy cleaning," he said.

There were some odds and ends of boards, and Diego knew where Mr. Ricardo kept his hand tools. The tools were old but well taken care of. Diego was surprised that he knew how to use them. He'd never made anything from wood before but he had watched his father. The men's prison in Cochabamba had a woodworking workshop where the prisoners could make dog houses and furniture to sell and earn money for food. Diego hadn't been allowed to do anything except sweep up the wood chips, but he'd learned a lot by watching.

Joining the corners was difficult. The old boards were a little uneven at the ends, and Diego couldn't figure out how to hold the boards together at right angles. He finally solved the problem by hammering a small piece of wood into one of the larger ones, which gave the other board a larger surface to attach to.

"I think this will work," he said as the new pen began to take shape. It was good to be useful. He liked to work, especially when the people he was working for were kind.

"Of course he can stay with us," Mrs. Ricardo had said that very first evening Diego appeared out of the jungle – filthy, scared and hungry.

"Who is he? We know nothing about him," Bonita said. They knew he'd been in the coca pits, and that his parents were in prison in Cochabamba. Beyond that they hadn't pressed.

"He's a boy in trouble," her mother said.

"Or he's a boy bringing trouble," Bonita said,

clamping a glare on her face as she watched him gulp down her mother's good soup, his first food in ages. He spooned it in so quickly that he nearly missed his mouth one time, and soup dribbled down his chin. "We should make him tell us what he is running from or send him on his way. He'll just eat up everything we work for."

"I can work, too," Diego said, as her parents told Bonita to hush. Bonita stopped talking but she didn't stop glaring, her face full of suspicion and scorn. "I can work," he said again, but he was weak from hunger, fear and thirst, from being lost in the jungle and spending so long in the coca pits.

Diego worried that Bonita might be right, that he wouldn't be able to earn his keep. There were times in the first few days when it seemed as if fatigue and grief would overwhelm him, and he'd never surface again.

Mrs. Ricardo seemed to understand this. Whenever he felt about to go under, she would give him something small to do. "Diego, help me peel the potatoes," or, "The eggs need gathering," or, "Let's spread all the blankets in the sun to air them out."

Deborah Ellis

Work helped. So did food, and many cups of hot coca tea, and the regular family life that went on around him. It even helped that Bonita didn't like him. It made everything more normal, some-how.

With each day he grew stronger. His fingers remembered how to dig down into the earth, how to tug out the weeds by their roots and snap the beans off their stems. He remembered how to act around the animals, how to feed and water them and keep their pens clean. The don-key seemed to like him. The llama seemed to hate him, but the llama hated everybody, so Diego fit right in.

"Diego! Come help me!" Mrs. Ricardo called from the edge of the clearing.

Diego hid the pen behind some bushes. He'd finish it later. He swung Santo up on to his back and ran toward the sound of Mrs. Ricardo's voice. She was standing by a whole pile of anu — giant tasty roots with little green leaves and small yellow flowers still attached.

"We'll have salad, and we'll have stew," Mrs. Ricardo said. "Can you help me carry this back? We have work to do."

For the next couple of hours Diego helped Mrs. Ricardo wash and chop the roots and greens. She wore a bowler hat and pollera skirts like his own mother, although the patterns were different. Diego could easily pretend it was his own mama he was working beside, enjoying the warmth of the sun and the beauty of the day.

The beauty faded a little when Bonita came home early. Her long dark hair was gathered in thick braids, and she wore an old shirt and trousers of her father's, arms rolled up and legs hemmed. She had the none-too-happy Martino by the wrist.

"I wanted to play football," Martino complained as soon as he saw his mother.

"You're too young to stay in the village by yourself," Bonita said. "I told you that."

"You're back early," Mrs. Ricardo said, handing Bonita a knife to chop the anu. Martino scampered off to sulk among the chickens. Diego decided he would get him to help with the new pen, to cheer him up.

"There's a teacher's strike," Bonita said. "Miss Gravas wasn't going to join it, but no one did their homework and everyone was being bad, so she said, 'I'm not being paid enough for this,' and walked out."

"Teachers have the right to make a decent wage," Mrs. Ricardo said.

Bonita didn't agree or disagree. "I tried to keep order after she left, but everyone just ran out, as if some big holiday had been declared. Including Martino."

"Maybe the strike will be settled quickly," Mrs. Ricardo said.

"I need to go to a real school," Bonita said. "Miss Gravas is okay with the younger kids, and with the stupid ones, but I'm too smart for her, and she doesn't know enough."

Diego laughed out loud, then tried to cover up his laugh with a cough. He was picturing Bonita, her braids as stiff as her frown, glaring up at her teacher and making the teacher afraid to say anything.

"Do you have something to say?" Bonita asked, acknowledging him directly for the first time that day.

Diego held his tongue and bent low over his chopping. Bonita was skilled at reminding him he was just a guest — an unwelcome one, in her view — and not a member of the family.

"If the coca crop is good," Mrs. Ricardo said, "and if we all stay healthy, maybe we can find you a better school."

"There are good schools in Cochabamba," Diego said, glad to know something Bonita didn't. "You can get scholarships. That means someone else will pay your fees, if you're smart. I have a scholarship."

"Clearly it didn't do you a lot of good," Bonita mumbled.

"A scholarship!" Mrs. Ricardo exclaimed. "Wouldn't that be fine, Bonita? My little Bonita, an important scholar in an important school!"

Mrs. Ricardo had such a gentle way of poking fun at bad moods, it was impossible for even Bonita to be miserable around her for long.

Diego's spirits dropped, though, as he thought about his own school. The agency that ran a drop-in center for children of prisoners had worked hard to get him in there. Now he wondered if the school would take him back — if he ever got home again.

To distract himself, he left Bonita and Mrs. Ricardo to finish chopping the anu and called Martino over to work with him on the new guinea pig pen.

"What's that?" Bonita asked, coming over. "You shouldn't waste our lumber."

"Just old scraps," Diego said. "It's a new pen for the guinea pigs. An idea I had."

"It will never fit under the stove," she said, examining it. "Did you measure?"

"Of course," Diego said, although he hadn't, and he had a few nervous moments until Bonita grudgingly admitted that it would fit.

"Those boards aren't very good," she said.

"They're the best I could find."

"Well, they'll never work." She had to add her own stamp by mixing up some mud and straw and filling the gaps. Martino and Santo enjoyed helping with this part, even with Bonita bossing them every two minutes.

By the time Mr. Ricardo came home, Diego had the mud washed off himself and the two little boys, and the new guinea pig pen was drying by the fire.

"This way we can pull it out to clean it,"

Bonita explained to her father, taking full credit for the project.

"Our guinea pigs will have the finest home in all of Bolivia," Mr. Ricardo said, but the smile didn't quite reach his eyes.

"What's wrong?" Mrs. Ricardo asked.

Mr. Ricardo took out his pouch of coca leaves and slowly counted out some to chew before he answered.

"The army is destroying coca crops again," he said. "On farms just on the other side of the valley. Word is passing from neighbor to neighbor."

"Is our crop ready to harvest?" Bonita asked. "We could sell it before they come here." Diego knew she was thinking of school.

"We will have to work hard," Mr. Ricardo said. "We'll have to bring it in ourselves. All the families around here will be doing the same thing, so they will have no help to spare."

"I'll help," Diego said.

"Do you mind staying home from school for a few days?" Mr. Ricardo asked Bonita.

"There's a teachers' strike," her mother said. "Perfect timing. We'll all work."

Deborah Ellis

Some of the worry left Mr. Ricardo's face. "We'll start in the morning."

They had the anu root for supper, boiled up on the fire with purple potatoes and flavored with the mint marigold that grew wild around the house.

The family had no electricity, and their supply of kerosene for the lamps had run out. When the sun went down, Bonita tried to read by the light of the dying cookfire but soon gave up.

They all went to bed early. They would have a long day tomorrow.

CHAPTER TWO

Diego woke up with a start, breathing heavily and sweating as if he'd been running. He thought he had screamed, but maybe he hadn't. Around him the Ricardo family slept undisturbed on their pallets. The scream must have been contained inside his head.

Gently he slid out from the blanket he shared with Martino and Santo, crossed the small one-room hut and unlatched the door. He heard the guinea pigs shuffling around in their new pen.

If only everything were that easy to fix.

Diego stepped outside into the Bolivian night full of the sounds of insects and night birds. He wasn't afraid of the dark. Bad things could just as easily happen when the sun shone. The sun had been shining when his parents were arrested. The sun had been shining when Mando was killed.

The cool air calmed him. He walked to the animal pen. The llama turned away, but the donkey trotted up to say hello. Diego ran his hands through its mane and blew gently in its ears.

He was fine now. He was alive and, thanks to the Ricardos, he was getting strong again. He'd find a way soon to make money – maybe in the village – and he would find some way to get home, with money in his pockets.

With a final rub of the donkey's ears, Diego turned around to go back to bed.

Bonita was standing in his way.

"Tell me now," she said. "What trouble are you bringing to my family?"

Diego looked down and saw she was pointing that old rusty rifle of hers at him. She'd found it in the bush, dropped by some forgotten soldier during some forgotten war. Even if it could shoot, the family had no bullets.

"What have you done?" she said again. "What are you running from?"

"I killed a man," Diego said, before he even

knew he was going to say anything. "He was a gringo, responsible for the death of my friend. I left him to die alone in the jungle."

As he spoke the simple words of the awful story, Diego felt calm, as if he was giving a report in school.

He didn't tell her how frightened he'd been. He didn't talk about how sad he felt whenever he thought of Mando. Bonita was smart. She'd know.

She kept looking at him. "Is anyone after you now?"

"I didn't see anyone else. His men probably think we're both dead."

"More money for them," Bonita said. Diego was right. She was smart. She lowered the rifle, then raised it again. "What about the police? Or the army? Will they come after you?"

"They were after Smith," Diego said. "I don't think they'd care if they found out he's dead."

"So, no reward for turning you in," Bonita said, lowering the rifle again and keeping it lowered this time. "I'm just thinking of my family. I don't know you."

"You could get to know me," Diego suggested.

"You won't be here that long," said Bonita, as she turned away. "I'm going back to bed. Some of us have to work in the morning."

A moment later, Diego heard her screech.

It made him laugh. Number twelve guinea pig had been found.

* * *

Diego loved every minute of the next few days. The family had nearly a hectare of coca bushes. All the leaves had to be picked, spread out to dry, then bundled into sacks and taken to the market.

Diego wore a long deep basket around his neck, handwoven by Mrs. Ricardo from grasses and vines. He learned how to pick the little green leaves with both hands, plucking them from their stems and dropping them in the basket.

"Don't take the tiny ones," Mrs. Ricardo said. "Give them a chance to grow. Pick only what's ready."

Diego worked hard, and he worked fast. He and Bonita were in an undeclared race to see who could fill the most baskets.

"I want to keep picking," Bonita called back when her mother called her to help prepare a meal. Mrs. Ricardo brought food out to them. Bonita and Diego ate while standing, shoving in cold potatoes and cornmeal and swallowing it all down with cold coca tea. They eyed each other through the branches to make sure one didn't start working before the other.

Mrs. Ricardo watched them for a few moments, rolled her eyes, shook her head and took their tea mugs back to the house.

Martino was picking leaves with Mr. Ricardo. He was still too young to really understand what was going on, except that he was being made to waste a perfectly good teachers' strike with days full of work.

Even Santo was pressed into work, helping Mrs. Ricardo spread the picked leaves on the drying sheets.

"Our coca goes to the market, for use by campesinos who don't grow their own," Mr. Ricardo said. "We don't sell it to the people who turn it into that white powder, that stuff they burn their brains with up north. Our coca is much too good for that." They were sitting by the fire eating vegetable stew left over from the previous night.

"Maybe some of it will end up in the prisons where my mother and father live," Diego said. "There are women there who sell coca to the other prisoners. Maybe my mother and father will chew some of this coca."

Hearing the words come out of his mouth made him sad and homesick, even for the prison. He threw some dried grass on to the fire and watched it flame up in the embers.

"You need to get back to your family," Mr. Ricardo said. "You work so hard, we will be sad to see you go, but you don't belong to us. We will give you the money from the sale of two sacks of coca. That should help you get back to your parents."

Diego's jaw dropped. Just like that, he had his way home. He tried to say thank you, but his eyes began to tear up, and he couldn't find the words.

Bonita made a funny noise — it was her school money Diego was taking — but she said nothing. Her parents had made a decision and that was that.

Diego wondered how much a bus ticket to Cochabamba would cost. Maybe he could hitch a ride — or several rides — instead, and save the coca money to give to his mother to pay for the fines she'd been given because of his carelessness. He pictured himself alone at the side of the road, waving at cars, hoping they'd give him a ride. It made him feel lonely. He picked up Santo and tried not to think about having to leave.

The next three days were more of the same, although it was difficult to keep up the pace he and Bonita had started. One day was especially hot, and Mrs. Ricardo insisted they take a break.

"Take the little ones for a swim," she said. "They're getting bored and cranky."

Not far up the hill, the stream widened into a deep pool.

"Papa and I spent last summer digging this out," Bonita said. "You're lucky we're letting you use it."

They stripped to their underclothes. Bonita went in first, hitting the surface of the water with a fistful of branches.

"To scare away the snakes," she said.

Diego felt that a dangerous sort of job like that should really be his, but Bonita wouldn't hear of it.

"You wouldn't do it right," she said, even though the job, as far as Diego could see, was just a matter of making as much noise in the water as possible.

Bonita just likes knowing things that I don't, he thought, and he left her to it.

The water was cold and refreshing, tumbling down from the mountains. Diego put Santo on his shoulders, dipping down lower and lower as the little boy squealed and screeched. Martino found a stick and they played stick-toss in the water, each one trying to make the stick land with as much splash as possible.

"Corina would love it here," Diego said, holding Santo by the stomach so he could kick his legs and pretend to swim. "She was born in the prison. I take her out to the square where there are gardens and fountains, but it's not like this."

"I can't imagine being locked up," Bonita said. "There are things I can't do, but there are reasons, like we don't have the money or I'm not old enough. I can't imagine having to do what

Sacred Leaf   33

someone tells me to, just because they're a guard and I have to obey them."

"I wasn't really a prisoner," Diego tried to explain. "My mother is, and my father, but not me."

"You lived in the prison. You had to obey the guards. What else is a prisoner? After being free, how could you go back in there again?"

That was one question Diego tried hard to avoid thinking about. He'd been out in the world now for many weeks, sleeping under the canopy of the jungle, seeing the sky, dealing with criminals and being scared and hungry, but also doing good work and being his own man.

Could he go back to sharing a narrow bed with his mother and sister in the dingy, tiny cell? Using the stinking toilets? Lining up for the morning count? Scrambling with the other boys for the good taxi jobs, the ones that paid two bolivianos instead of just one?

"But that's where my family is," Diego said. "Could you leave your family?"

"You already left yours," she said. "My family wouldn't want me to live in a prison."

Diego was so angry he almost dropped Santo right in the water.

"*My* parents didn't want me to live in prison. How can you think they did? They were put in prison for smuggling coca paste, something they didn't do! You think you know everything, but you don't know anything."

Diego stomped out of the pond – hard to do, since water is not made for stomping – taking Santo out with him. Santo was crying because of the shouting and because he didn't want to leave the water and because he was too small to do anything about it. Diego was going to leave him on the mud bank, but he wouldn't have done that to Corina, so he scooped up the little boy's clothes and carried him back to the coca bushes. He plopped the red-faced Santo into Mrs. Ricardo's arms and went back to work, too angry to explain.

How could he be angry at his own parents? They'd never been to school, had to scramble for every centavo just to live. There was no money to pay a lawyer to fight the charges. They did their best for him, made sure he ate and behaved and went to school. How could he be angry with them?

And yet he was. He thought of those high

walls of the prison, and his anger made him work harder, even when he knew that his hard work was making his return to that prison all the more possible.

Bonita was soon back picking coca leaves, too, but she chose a bush far away from him.

Mrs. Ricardo saw both of them, rolled her eyes, shook her head again and went back to work.

CHAPTER THREE

The harvest was in.

Some of it was bagged and ready to transport. Most was still drying, spread out on big sheets of plastic.

If even a tiny bit of moisture remained in the leaves, they would go moldy when they were bundled up. Every now and then, Martino or Santo would shuffle through the leaves, whooshing them around with their feet to make sure the sun reached every leaf. Diego thought he'd like to make that whooshing sound, too, but he couldn't, not in front of Bonita. After all, he was a serious working man.

While they waited for the crop to dry, the family and Diego stood on the edge of the sheets of leaves and said out loud what they saw in their dreams.

"A real football," said Martino.

"School," said Bonita.

"New shoes for all of you," said Mrs. Ricardo.

"New farm tools," Mr. Ricardo said. "Lumber to repair the house and the animal pens."

"Home," said Diego. This time he didn't see the prison walls, or the cramped cell, or the angry guards. He only saw his mother and his father and his little sister – and himself, returning home triumphantly with his pockets full of money.

"Staring at these leaves won't make them dry any faster," Mrs. Ricardo said suddenly, waving her family into action. "Did everyone suddenly run out of chores to do? Would you like me to find you some?"

There was always something to do on the farm. Diego fetched water for the animals and helped Mr. Ricardo muck out the stalls.

He was giving Martino a ride on the donkey when Bonita called up, "If you've finished playing, I could use your help in the house."

Martino made fun of her all the way back

Deborah Ellis

down to the hut. Diego tried hard not to laugh as the little boy mimicked his big sister's walk and the way she tossed her head when she was impatient.

"We need to sweep the walls," she said, handing Diego a broom. "To make sure there are no kissing bugs."

Martino giggled and started to make loud kissing noises at Bonita.

His sister tried to ignore him. "It's a beetle that can give you chagas disease. It lives in thatched roofs like ours. My parents keep saying they'll get a tin roof but there's never enough money — especially since we keep taking in strays." She gave Diego a glare that told him to get busy.

Diego ran the broom over the clay walls and wooden rafters, then helped Martino carry the rag rugs into the yard to shake.

"Martino!" Bonita yelled from inside. She rushed out holding a little cardboard box.

"Those are mine!" Martino said, leaping up. Bonita held it out of his reach.

"He's been collecting the bugs we're trying to get rid of," she told Diego. "Look!"

Diego peered at the dozen or so bugs scrambling around inside.

"They're mine!" Martino said. "I'm going to race them!"

"How many times do we have to tell you?" Bonita tossed the beetles into the smoldering cookfire, then tossed the empty box on the coals, too. It started to smoke, then flamed up.

Diego gave the rugs a vigorous shake. Chagas was dangerous, he remembered from science class. Martino needed to find something safer to play with.

He was about to move on to the pillows and blankets when a soft *thump-thump* sound reached his ears. It took him a moment to identify it. Then, as it came closer and became louder, he knew.

Only one thing could make such a noise.

No, he thought. No.

And then the helicopter was upon them, giant and green, propellers thumping as it hovered over the small farm.

The little ones screamed and started to run. Mrs. Ricardo snatched them up in her arms so they wouldn't run off into the forest. She went

Deborah Ellis

down on her knees and turned their wailing faces to her chest to shield them from the flying debris stirred up by the propellers. Diego watched help- lessly as the drying coca leaves took to the air like butterflies and scattered to the four winds.

The helicopter landed in the family's yard. At the same time, pick-up trucks sped up the dirt road. Soldiers spilled out, pointing their weapons and trampling the vegetable gardens under their heavy boots. The propellers slowed to a halt, and for a moment there was silence in the clearing as the soldiers and the family stared at each other.

Then there was a horrible yell, and Diego saw Bonita run out of the hut, her old useless rifle pointed at the soldiers around the helicopter. Diego heard the soldiers step forward, heard them raise their rifles to firing position.

Then he heard another yell, this one rising from his own throat.

"NOOOOO!"

With great leaps he crossed the yard, slammed into Bonita and knocked her to the ground. The rusty rifle spun away. He lay down hard while she tried to fight him off.

"Lower your guns. She's just a child," a man said.

Diego heard the soldiers relax, returning their rifles to their shoulders. A sergeant was taking charge.

"We are under orders to take your coca," he told the Ricardos, "and that's what we're going to do."

"You have no right!" Mr. Ricardo said, stomping up to them, only to be held back by the point of a gun. "You wait until we do all the work of harvesting. Then you come and take what we've worked for."

"Grow food," the sergeant said. "Grow vegetables."

"We grow vegetables," Mrs. Ricardo said, the children still crying in her arms. "You're standing in our onion patch. But we can't wear onions. We can't pay for school books with onions."

Bonita stopped fighting him, so Diego let her up. She punched him hard before taking Santo from her mother. Diego understood. He'd seen plenty of prisoners hit each other because it was too dangerous to hit a guard.

The soldiers were loading the sacks of coca

on to the back of the pick-up truck. Others went over the farm with axes and shovels, cutting down and digging up the coca bushes the family had carefully grown and tended. They trampled on the sweet potato plants and broke down the stalks of growing corn. They went inside the small stone hut, and Diego heard the sounds of crashing and banging.

"There are no coca bushes growing inside our home!" Mr. Ricardo shouted. "Why are you doing this?"

"Maybe you are hiding coca paste in there," the sergeant said. "Maybe you even have cocaine."

"We just have things we need to live," cried Mrs. Ricardo. "Don't you have families? Don't you have shame?"

"Stay back and we'll get this done," said the sergeant.

The Ricardo farm was small. Destroying it didn't take long. Soon the trucks were heaped with hacked-up coca bushes and sacks of dried leaves.

Bonita's school, Martino's football, the repairs on the farm — and Diego's ticket home — all disappeared.

Now Diego had no way to return to his family with money in his pockets, and no way to make up for the fear and worry he'd caused his parents.

Helplessness was bitter in his mouth. It soured his stomach and pushed out all caution.

Bonita's rifle was on the ground. The soldiers had looked at its rust and broken parts, laughed and tossed it away.

Diego picked it up now, holding it by the snout. He lunged at the nearest truck. The soldiers were smoking and laughing, their work done. Diego ran and swung, smashing headlights and bumpers, hammering the barrel of the rifle into the hood of the truck, trying to hit clear through to the engine. If the truck couldn't go, it couldn't carry away their coca.

Diego banged at the truck, denting metal. He kept swinging even as the soldiers dropped their cigarettes and came after him, not caring who or what he hit.

There were shouts and curses as the soldiers tried to grab him and were hit in the face, legs or chest. Finally they attacked him as a group, and took him down.

Diego hit dirt, face first. It got up his nose and into his eyes. He could hear the Ricardos yelling. Even Bonita was cursing the soldiers for hurting him. But the soldiers didn't care. They held him down and yanked back his arms, winding twine so tightly around his wrists that his hands began to burn and then lost sensation. He tasted dirt and blood and felt the weight of men kneeling on his back.

"Your son is under arrest," the sergeant said. "He assaulted my men."

Diego waited for the Ricardos to say, "He's not our son," but they didn't. Instead they said, "He is small and you are big. You are arresting him? What type of people are you?"

The soldiers didn't respond. They lifted Diego up by his arms. It hurt a lot to be lifted like that, with sharp pain stretching all across his back. He was ashamed to find that he was crying. His face was wet with dirt and tears, and his shirt was red with blood from his nose.

Diego's head was ringing from too much going on. The Ricardos were pleading, the little ones were crying, and Bonita was yelling. The sergeant was barking orders. Diego kicked and squirmed, but the soldiers were bigger and they lifted him into the back of the truck. He was dumped among the sacks of leaves and murdered coca bushes. A branch from a bush poked him in the eye.

He was too angry to keep still. He worked his way to his feet and tried to jump off the back of the truck, but the soldiers blocked his way.

"Whoa! Slow down!" one of them said. "We won't hurt you. Just settle down."

Diego couldn't push through them, so he got as far away as possible. He wiggled his way through the uprooted coca bushes until he was wedged between the cab of the truck and the mound of coca sacks. He looked back at the Ricardo family standing together, the parents' arms around their children. They were all crying now.

Diego knew they were crying because of the lost crop and the lost dreams that were going away with it. He also knew they were crying for him. He'd only been with them for a week, but he knew that they liked him as much as he liked them.

The helicopter started up again, the noise and propellers creating a powerful storm of wind.

Deborah Ellis

"Thank you!" Diego shouted out to the Ricardos as the soldiers climbed into the trucks and they started to drive away.

He couldn't even raise his hands to wave goodbye.

CHAPTER FOUR

The pick-up truck moved down the road. It
wasn't a road made for trucks. It was a path better suited to llamas and donkeys, full of ruts and
rocks and places where the bush had taken over.

Diego's eyes stung from the dirt and tears he
was unable to wipe away. He was wedged in
among the coca sacks. They cushioned him as
the truck rolled over the uneven road. Low
branches brushed his face.

As the shock of his arrest wore off, his panic
rose. He couldn't go to jail! He couldn't be
locked up like his parents, only ever being able
to see the sky from the prison courtyard.

The truck stopped and started, eventually
turning onto a smoother road and picking up

speed. It wasn't long before it turned again, and Diego was bumped around the truck bed as before.

Eventually the truck came to a stop and the motor was turned off. Diego heard more voices and the sound of music coming from a radio. He smelled wood smoke and cooking. He got ready to bolt.

The soldiers got out of the truck, lowered the flap on the back, and hands reached in for Diego.

He was ready, but there were too many against him. They held him up off the ground and laughed as his legs tried to run in the air.

"What's going on?" A tall man in a clean uniform strode up to the soldiers holding Diego. "What's this kid doing here?"

"Assault, Captain," one of the soldiers said. "He went after us with a rifle."

"He shot at you?"

"Well, no, the rifle was old and no good. He hit us with it."

Diego stopped struggling. They put him on his feet but kept a strong grip on his shoulders and arms.

Diego's taxi skills were finally starting to kick

in. Be watchful and ready. Keep your eyes open for the best advantage.

"He hit you with an old, useless rifle." The captain sounded unimpressed.

"He hit our truck, too," a soldier added. "Broke a headlight."

"And so you brought him here. Does this look like a playground?"

Diego looked beyond them to the small group of nylon tents, the tarps stretched between the trees to provide rain shelter over the cooking and eating area. Trucks and jeeps were parked along the edge of the camp. He saw lines of laundry, stores of food and bottles of drinking water.

He also saw, off to the side, the sacks of coca leaves and the ripped-out coca bushes taken from raids on farms just like the Ricardos'.

"What's your name?" the captain asked, bending down so he could talk straight to Diego.

"Diego."

"Your parents shouldn't be growing coca, Diego. Don't they know that?"

"They don't just *grow* coca," one of the soldiers said. "Look at his legs."

They lifted him up again so his legs dangled

in the air. Diego took advantage of the moment to kick the soldier in the stomach. The other men laughed as the soldier bent over, winded and in pain.

"You've been stomping coca," the captain said. Weeks in the coca pits had bleached all the color out of Diego's feet and legs. The sores were healing, but they were still there – red blotches on washed-out skin. "Your parents are monsters, making you do that. Don't they know it rots your skin away?"

"They're not my parents," Diego said. He'd meant to defend the Ricardos, but the wrong words came out. "They had nothing to do with the pit. They took me in. I ran away from the pit. The men there killed my friend."

"Killed your friend?" That got the captain's attention. "Where was this? Can you show us?"

"There was jungle," Diego said, "and a rope bridge, and a little village with a shop." As he talked, he knew he'd never find it. He'd slept on the trip there from Cochabamba. Then there was the terrifying helicopter ride with Smith, and another dash through the jungle. He had no way to prove his story.

"Where are your parents, then?" the captain asked.

Diego held his tongue. He knew he'd broken the law by working in the coca pits. What if the army made his parents spend more time in prison because of what he'd done? He wasn't going to make things worse. He wasn't going to answer any more questions until he knew exactly what those answers would cost him.

He set his lips firmly tight and gave the captain the sort of glare he'd wanted to give the prison guards all those years but was afraid to.

The captain just laughed. "I wish the rest of you were as tough as this kid," he said to the other soldiers. "Then the Bolivian army would conquer all of South and Central America and not stop until we reached the White House. Wouldn't the gringos be surprised to see us there? We'll take the boy back to that farm tomorrow and search for that pit. If there are no signs of it, we'll know he's telling at least some truth."

The captain gave orders to unload the coca and to find Diego a secure place where he couldn't get away.

The soldiers first tied Diego to a tree, with the rope going around his middle so he had to keep standing. The captain called them idiots, cut the twine from around Diego's wrists and sat him down at the table in the kitchen area. He tied one of Diego's ankles to a leg of the table.

"If he gets away, I'll blame you, not him," he told his men. "Do your job properly." Diego saw the captain pass a signal to the older man who was cooking nearby.

"Hungry?" the cook asked.

Diego never turned down food. He'd been without it too often.

He nodded. A warm empanada was placed in front of him, and he gobbled it down.

"I see you like my empanadas," the cook said.

"They're good," Diego agreed.

"I bake them on the fire. You wouldn't think that was possible, would you?"

Diego had never thought about it. "No."

"Let me show you. You seem like a cultured fellow, interested in good food and the finer things of life."

Diego laughed.

The cook's hands danced about, spooning

chopped meat and vegetables into squares of pastry.

"The men here don't know an ear of corn from the ear of a pig. They want hot, fast and plenty. They swallow without even chewing. They don't care what they eat, so I can experiment. I'm going to write a cookbook when I retire. Foods of Bolivia. Do you think it will sell?"

Diego nodded. He wiggled his bound foot, testing the strength of the captain's knot. The cook kept talking, but he watched Diego out of the corner of his eye. Diego was used to judging the alertness and temperament of guards, and he knew he was being watched. It didn't stop him from trying to wiggle out of his bindings.

The cook put a fresh batch of empanadas in a makeshift oven of folded foil and pot lids. He never stopped talking, telling Diego how to prepare and bake a monkey, what type of snakes could be added to stew and disguised as chicken, different herbs in different parts of Bolivia.

"If only we'd go to war again with Chile," he said wistfully. "We could get back our access to the ocean, and I'd have fresh shellfish to work with."

The baked empanadas were set aside to cool. They'd be given to the men on night patrol, the cook said.

Diego was allowed to sit with the men for supper. The food was much better than what he was used to. Rice, beans, corn and chicken. He ate as much as he was given. He didn't know what was ahead, but it wasn't likely to include food like this.

The soldiers grumbled about eating with a prisoner, and a kid at that.

"Take your plates elsewhere, then," the captain said. "This kid showed more spirit and loyalty today than all the rest of you have since you came under my command."

"Maybe you should draft him," a soldier said. "He can take my place."

"Mine, too," several men echoed.

"Or you could hire me," Diego said suddenly. "I could work for you. For pay," he added. "I could run errands, help the cook, keep things tidy." He counted off the chores on his fingers.

"You think a kid like you is tough enough to work with soldiers like us?" one of the men jeered.

"What's so tough about you?" Diego asked. "All you do is rip up coca bushes and steal from farmers. Big, tough soldiers."

"We go after the coca farmers because they're easy to find," the captain said. "We have to stop the flow of cocaine to North America. The United States government gives Bolivia money to do this. Bolivia is poor. We need this money."

"Money's no good if it makes you do bad things," said Diego.

"Now he's an expert in government, too," said one of the soldiers, shoveling in more rice.

"Perhaps you have a better idea," the captain said to Diego. "I grew up in this territory. So did most of my men. You think we want to make our neighbors poor?"

"Catch the bad guys," Diego said.

The captain laughed, but it was a laugh without any humor in it.

"Catch the bad guys. The bad guys who have more money than we do, more planes, more helicopters, more friends in high places. You wouldn't understand this, Diego, because you're only a boy, but just because someone is in a position of power and authority doesn't automatically mean he's a good person."

Diego knew all about that. He'd seen guards steal from prisoners.

"I didn't join the army to rip up plants and scare good families," the captain said. "You find me a way to catch the real bad guys and I'll do it."

The soldiers left the table as soon as their plates were empty. The cook poured himself and the captain some coffee and poured Diego a mug of tostada.

"Where are your parents?" the captain asked again.

"In prison," Diego finally admitted. "In Cochabamba."

"You were living with them in the prison?"

"In San Sebastian Women's Prison."

"Do they know where you are and what you've been doing?"

Diego shook his head and stared down at the table. He pictured himself walking into the women's prison with nothing to show for his time away. The guards and the other prisoners would see him for what he was – just a dumb kid

Sacred Leaf   57

who never did anything right. Sure his parents would be glad to see him, but then what?

He took a big swallow of the warm, sweet drink to keep himself from crying. There was still the debt to pay, and no way to pay it.

Diego was put on a spare cot in the cook's tent for the night. He was handcuffed to the frame of the cot with real handcuffs, not just a rope he could try to untie.

"It's for your own good," the cook said, as he turned down the flame on the kerosene lantern. "There are too many things out there that can hurt a boy on his own."

Diego was too miserable to answer. He lay in the dark, listening to the noises of the military camp settling down for the night. Across the tent, the cook slept on his own cot and snored.

Hoping the sound of the snoring would cover up the sounds of his sobs, Diego cried.

CHAPTER FIVE

Diego was wakened by the sound of jeeps revving their engines and the noise of heavy boots running through the camp. His handcuffs had been removed some time during the night, and the cook's cot was empty.

He poked his head outside the tent.

"Let's go!" the captain yelled to his men. "Load up!"

"What's happened?" one of the soldiers asked.

"The cocaleros are blocking the highways," the captain said. "Get Diego into a truck!"

"Diego? Who's Diego?"

"The boy! Put the boy in a truck. Maybe we can use him."

Diego started running, but he was no match for the soldiers, and he landed face-down in the dirt. In the next instant the cook was there, threatening the soldiers with his frying pan. The soldiers apologized, picked Diego up, dusted him off and led him over to one of the trucks.

"What are you doing?" Diego asked, as he was lifted up into the back of a pick-up truck. "Where are we going?"

"Just following orders," said the soldier, getting into the truck beside him.

The convoy of pick-ups started to head out of the camp. The cook ran up with a bundle full of still-warm empanadas.

"Don't share them with the lads," he told Diego. "They're all for you."

More soldiers climbed into the back of the truck, squishing Diego against the side wall. He clutched the bundle of pastries to his chest with one hand and held on to the side of the pick-up with the other. The truck lurched into action and joined the line of military vehicles heading out on the road.

In spite of not knowing what was happening, Diego was enjoying himself. He was no longer handcuffed, the good Bolivian sun was shining down on him, and all around was green and beautiful. He'd wait and watch out for his next best chance.

The truck passed through a small village, slowed down, then came to a complete stop. Diego leaned out to try to see what was happening, but his view was blocked by the trucks ahead. The captain's jeep pulled out of the line and drove down the side of the highway.

Diego couldn't see what was going on, but all the car horns blasting away told him a lot of traffic was being held up.

"Bloody cocaleros!" One of the soldiers next to Diego spat over the side of the truck. "This was supposed to be my day off."

Then the captain's jeep pulled up beside the truck, and the captain ordered the convoy to follow him to the front of the line. They drove down the wrong lane of the highway, passing cars with horns honking, trucks full of lumber and cattle, and a bus full of people hanging out of the windows, yelling complaints.

The truck reached the front of the stalled line of traffic, and stopped.

And then it was before them.

Stretched across the road was a line of people sitting on the pavement, not letting anything pass. In front of them was a barrier of logs and branches.

Behind the first barricade were more people dragging more branches on to the road. Some were stringing tarps between branches to make a shelter. Diego saw children and babies, old people and folks in between.

And then he saw someone he knew.

"Mrs. Ricardo! Mrs. Ricardo!" He waved and hollered, but Mrs. Ricardo didn't seem to hear. There was a lot of noise from people yelling curses and banging on their car horns, and from the cocaleros yelling out chants and slogans.

"We want justice! We want justice!"

He watched the captain walk alone up to the front line of protesters. A small group of men and women stepped out of the blockade and walked up to meet him. Diego watched the captain listen to names and shake everyone's hands. He couldn't hear what was being said, but he watched the protesters talk, saw the captain nod, then wave his arm at the line of backed-up cars and trucks.

The protesters shook their heads.

This went on for awhile longer, with more gestures and more discussions. Then the captain shook hands all around again and walked back to the line of cars.

"Let's get this traffic turned around," he said.

"Where to?"

"Back to that village," the captain said. "A lot of people sitting out here in cars with nothing to do but get angry is not going to help anything. Move."

The soldiers had been trained to do many things, but traffic control was not one of them. Arguments broke out among the drivers and among the soldiers, with everyone adding to the noise with their own complaints and curses. Parents chased after children who had escaped from the cars during their long wait. Crates of chickens squawked and went crazy when one of the crates fell off the truck and broke open, sending birds in all directions. The line of vehicles became hopelessly confused and Diego, with a front-row seat in the back of the pick-up, enjoyed every minute. For a long while, everything the army tried to do to fix the problem only made it worse.

The captain looked completely humiliated at the incompetence of his men, and he finally called a halt to everything so they could meet and come up with a workable plan. After that the soldiers worked together and the cars were turned back.

With the cars and trucks gone, the stretch of highway became quieter. Even the chants of the protesters faded a bit. It was as though everyone needed a bit of a breather so they could be ready for whatever would happen next.

The military trucks and jeeps now spread themselves out to cover both lanes of the highway. They became another blockade. The two blockades were facing each other.

The captain went into the middle of the road and put his hands up for quiet. The protesters stopped their chants so that they could hear what he had to say.

"We have just made the area safer for you," he said. "We did this because we don't want anything bad to happen here. You are Bolivian, and we are Bolivian. I am sure that we can come to some agreement."

"Give us back our coca!" shouted one of the protesters. This resulted in cheers and several minutes of chants. The captain waited until they settled down again.

"You know I cannot do that. You ask me for something impossible. That's not the way to negotiate. We have made this area safe for you to protest. In return, I would like you to limit your protest to one hour."

This brought such a wave of laughter and jeers that Diego almost felt sorry for the captain.

"Bolivia does not have many highways," the captain shouted, trying to make himself heard. "Trucks and buses do not have choices. Think of commerce, think of the economy! Think of people needing to get from one place to another. If you shut down the road, you shut down a lot of Bolivia."

The chants drowned him out.

"We should just shoot them," said the soldier standing next to Diego. "Why does he waste time like this?"

"You're an idiot," said Diego. "You'll never

keep a girlfriend." He knew from spending time in the men's prison that this was a good way to insult another man. He got a swat on the side of his head for the remark, but it was worth it.

"There must be something you want that I can give you," shouted the captain as soon as he had the chance.

"You took away a boy yesterday," someone shouted. "We want him back."

"That's what this is about? The boy? You can have him." The captain took big quick strides to the truck where Diego was standing and lifted him to the ground.

He put his arm around Diego's shoulder and marched him to the line of protesters so quickly that there was no time for Diego to agree or dis-agree.

Mrs. Ricardo jumped out of the line, crying and hugging Diego as if he was her very own son. Mr. Ricardo was there, too, and Santo and Martino. Even Bonita looked happy to see him, although she turned her face away as soon as she saw Diego look at her.

A space was made for Diego in the first line of the blockade, right beside Mrs. Ricardo. He gave her the bundle of empanadas, which she passed to someone else, to be shared out later. She put her arm around him, and he nestled right into her, not caring that he was a little too old to have such a fuss made over him. He liked the fuss.

"You've got the boy," the captain said. "Now we need to clear this highway."

"We need our coca back," came the shout. The chants started again.

Diego joined in. It was fun to yell and chant, and maybe the chants would work. The captain would get fed up and return their coca. The Ricardos could sell their crop. Then Diego would have his share of the money, and he could go home.

The captain stood in the road for a few minutes trying to calm things down, but the chanting took on a life of its own. Diego yelled and slapped his knees, keeping time with the rhythm of the chants. He helped Santo, in Mrs. Ricardo's lap, clap along to the beat.

The captain turned away and walked back to his men. He held a brief meeting with his sergeants, then climbed up on to the back of his jeep in the middle of the road.

The chanting was so loud that Diego didn't hear the first order. He just saw the rifles come out and up as the men went into firing position.

The chanting stopped almost instantly. Around him everyone became very still. Mrs. Ricardo handed Santo to someone who took him behind the barricade, and Mr. Ricardo pushed Martino to the back. Diego could hear other small children back there laughing and playing some little kid game. He heard birds singing. And he saw the soldiers, their fingers on triggers, ready to shoot.

"This highway must be cleared!" the captain shouted into the silence. "I'm going to count to ten. We don't want to do this! I've asked you to move. If anyone gets hurt, you have brought it on yourselves."

Diego glanced at the faces of the people beside him. He saw fear, but no one moved.

"One!" shouted the captain.

"Bonita, get to the back," her father ordered.

"No," Bonita said, taking hold of her father's hand.

"Two!" shouted the captain.

"Diego, take Bonita to the back," Mr. Ricardo said.

Diego, wanting to obey, put his hand on Bonita's arm but took it off again when he was hit with her glare.

"Three!"

Diego sat back down on the line between Mrs. Ricardo and a man he didn't know. Mrs. Ricardo clasped Diego's hand in hers. Diego held the hand of the man sitting on the other side of him. He didn't know the man's name, but they were friends now.

The captain kept shouting numbers, loudly and slowly.

"Six!"

Diego heard people whisper the Hail Mary. He was too angry to pray.

At "Eight!" one of the soldiers lowered his rifle.

"Captain," he said, "I can't shoot these people. My own village is not far from here. Arrest me if you want, but I won't shoot." He jumped down off his truck and laid his rifle on the ground.

"Me, too, Captain," another private said. Half a dozen men put their rifles on the ground.

The count never got to ten.

"Lower your weapons!" the captain ordered.

"I don't get paid enough to do this, and neither do you. Someone higher up can take responsibility. Back in the trucks."

The men jumped back into the pick-up trucks, the motors were started, and one by one the convoy turned around and drove back down the highway.

The blockade erupted in a roar. Cheers and singing, hugging and dancing. Bonita even hugged Diego until she realized what she was doing and pushed him away.

"They will be back," an old woman said when the celebration had calmed down a bit. "We know they will be back, and we must be ready. Back to work."

Always, there was work. It was the one thing in life Diego could count on. Luckily he liked work, and he plunged right in, making himself useful.

CHAPTER SIX

"How did you find me?" Diego asked Mr. Ricardo as they worked together dragging a huge branch out of the forest.

"We didn't," said Mr. Ricardo. "We were just lucky."

"What would you have done if they hadn't let me go?" Diego asked.

"Why in the world would they want to keep you?" asked Bonita, coming along just in time to insult him. She helped them drag the branch onto the highway. "We'll need a lot more than this," she said, almost scolding Diego and her father for taking a moment to catch their breath. She went back into the forest ahead of them.

"Was she always like this?" Diego asked.

"Always," said Mr. Ricardo, smiling. "My Bonita will be president of Bolivia one day."

Diego didn't stop to consider whether that would be a good thing or a bad thing. He just got back to work.

A short while later a meeting was called. A man stood up to speak.

"It has been suggested that we move the blockade two hundred meters down the highway and take over the bridge. What does everybody think?"

This was the first of many, many meetings Diego was a part of. Everything needed to be discussed and voted on, and everyone — or so it seemed to Diego — had an opinion. This took some time, but in the end everyone agreed to move the blockade.

The bridge was long, stretching high over a wide, deep valley where a shallow river ran through it on a rocky bed. Hills of deep green forest rose up at each end, the south end of the highway flowing straight, then curving gently to the side. At the north end of the bridge, the highway rose up into a hill, then swerved around to follow the course of the river.

Deborah Ellis

The bridge gave the protesters a good vantage point. They could easily see what was coming from both directions.

They moved in groups, taking branches and blockade material down the hill with them. Some went ahead to clear the bridge of the cars that were already there, getting the drivers to move on through so that they'd be out of the way. Diego heard some curses, but also some calls of good luck from the drivers who were allowed to leave the bridge and continue north.

Once they were on the bridge, some protesters went right down to the south end and began setting up the blockade there, first by standing in the road, then with logs and branches as more people joined them. Diego ran up and down the highway, carrying and dragging things to the bridge, then dashing back to get another armful. He smiled at people he didn't know, and they smiled back.

Diego and the others went into the woods at the south end and carried branches and old logs to the bridge from the forest floor.

He had just dragged his third branch across the south end of the bridge when a call went up to reinforce the north end. Diego rushed to the far end of the bridge with the others. Cars were beginning to gather on the other side. One of the drivers was trying to push his way through the blockade. He leaned on the horn of his shiny red sports car and stuck his head out the window, cursing the protesters and trying to hit any of them who came close.

The cocaleros formed a solid wall of people in front of the car. Diego banged his fist on the hood the way some of the others were doing to get the driver to stop and turn around.

Still the driver moved forward. "Get out of my way or I'll step on the gas. I don't care how many of you peasants I kill!"

The driver was of Spanish background, with pale skin. He was not Quechua or Aymara. He and his clothes were shiny and bright, just like his car. He was from another world in Bolivia, the world with money.

The cocalero men leaned on his car, shouting for him to stop, trying to force him to go back.

"I'll kill you!" he shouted. "Lousy coca chewers. I'll run you all down!"

Diego saw one of the young cocaleros, a man

wearing a black baseball cap, take a small knife from the top of his boot. He went around to the driver's window and held the knife up to the man's face, grinning.

"Go ahead," taunted the driver. "Do it! You don't have the guts. Bloody cowards. Bloody cocaleros!" He spat the word, turning a proud label into a curse.

Diego saw the young man smile, give his knife blade a kiss, then kneel down out of sight. In the next instant, Diego heard the *szzzt* of air escaping from a tire.

There were cheers, and the other three tires were also quickly slashed as the young cocalero walked around the car from one tire to the other.

Still, the driver insisted on going forward. The protesters let him, laughing as they made way for him to roll on to the bridge on tires that flopped and wobbled on the wheel rims. In the middle of the bridge he gave up, shutting off the motor and grabbing the keys.

"Somebody will pay for this!" he shouted, getting out of his car.

He left the bridge, on foot.

Some of the young men were excited by the

fine, sleek car. They ran their hands over the smooth metal and started to argue over who could sit in the driver's seat. They opened the glove compartment and honked the horn. Being so close to such an expensive car made them forget why they were on the blockade in the first place.

Mrs. Ricardo and other women had their say.

"Pull the car off the bridge," they ordered. "It does not help us to have it here, and it will give people an excuse to attack us. We are farmers, not thugs or thieves. Give the man back his car."

It took a bit of persuading, but the young men obeyed. Ropes were attached, the car was put into neutral gear, and the cocaleros formed themselves into pushers and pullers.

Diego tried to get a spot as a pusher, but there was no room, so he scrambled to the other end of the car, took hold of a rope and pulled.

The car inched its way up the little hills that led away from the bridge. It was almost like the processions Diego had seen around the cathedral in Cochabamba during Holy Week, although with a rich man's car instead of a statue of the Virgin Mary.

They pushed and they pulled until they

Deborah Ellis

reached a spot where the car wouldn't roll. Then they stripped away the useless tires. Two tires went to one end of the bridge. Two went to the other.

"We need rocks," someone said. "There are lots of rocks down by the river."

On each side of the bridge there was a pathway that led down to the river. The protesters split up so that rocks could be brought up both sides.

Diego picked his way down the steep river bank to find a place in line. Rocks were passed from hand to hand like great rock snakes on each side of the river. Diego spotted Bonita working on the other side, and before his brain could stop it, his arm moved and he waved to her.

He almost dropped a rock on his foot when she waved back.

Diego lifted rocks until his arms and shoulders were burning with pain. Then he kept going until his legs were sore, too. He could have stepped out of line and taken a break — many did, old and young — but Bonita wasn't breaking, so of course neither did he.

Finally the call came that there were enough

rocks for now. The climb up the hill was painful. Diego needed a helping hand from one of the others. He hoped Bonita couldn't see.

"What happens now?" he asked someone.

"We wait," he was told. "The government can't leave this highway blockaded forever. There's no other way to get to Santa Cruz. They will have to give in to our demands."

Up on the bridge, people were breaking into groups.

"We have formed committees," Mr. Ricardo told Diego. "Do you know what committees are?"

"Sure," he said. "My mother is on three committees in her prison. She says it's the committees that get things done, and all the guards do is keep people locked up."

"We get things done here in committees, too," Mr. Ricardo said. "We need certain things to happen, like food and security and shelter, so we form committees to do those things. Otherwise it would be hard to figure out what to do, because we would all be trying to do everything."

Diego was certainly old enough to join a committee. He leaned against the railing of the bridge

Deborah Ellis

while Mr. Ricardo explained what the different committees were doing.

"Over there is the sign-painting committee. They are deciding what the signs and banners should say, and then they will paint the slogans on sheets and boards."

"Where will they get the paint?" Diego asked.

"I'm coming to that," Mr. Ricardo said. "There is also a food committee that will plan and prepare food for all of us. The security committee will find people to stand watch, and the communications committee is meeting now to draft a message that we can give to the press. You can be on that committee even if you can't read. You can speak your thoughts and someone will write them down."

Diego thought that committee sounded like too much talking.

Mr. Ricardo went on. "The construction committee will build latrines. There's an education committee, a daycare committee and a medical committee. And that's just to start," Mr. Ricardo grinned. "The work gets spread around so nobody has to do too much, and everybody feels they are a part of things."

Diego looked at the groups of farming families talking together all over the bridge.

"Where do they get the paint?" he asked again.

"That's the job of the runners committee," Mr. Ricardo said. "They find things we need, and they run errands for the other committees."

"That sounds like the place for me," Diego said. "Can you be on more than one committee?"

"You can, if you can keep your commitments. People will be counting on you, so don't take on more than you know you can do. What other committee interests you?"

"The security committee," Diego said. "Standing watch. Isn't that a little like being on guard?"

Mr. Ricardo smiled again. "It's very much like being on guard."

"Guard Diego," Diego said. He laughed with Mr. Ricardo, then the two of them got back to work.

CHAPTER SEVEN

As Diego worked, the bridge was transformed into a village.

With no one in charge barking orders, no one standing over people to make them work, no one bossing anyone else, the cocaleros decided among themselves what needed to be done and how to do it.

Mr. Ricardo was part of the security committee. He and the other members were very businesslike and got to the heart of the matter without a lot of discussion.

"We need to post watches at each barricade and make sure there are enough volunteers to change over every couple of hours."

Diego volunteered for one of the middle-of-the-night shifts, and no one told him that he wasn't old enough.

"There will be two or three people on watch at all times at each end of the bridge," Mr. Ricardo said. "More eyes will make us all safer."

The runners committee was a different story.

"What are you staring at?" Bonita asked, when Diego arrived at the group's first meeting.

"Is this the runners committee?" he asked, hoping it wasn't. Aside from Bonita, the other two members of the committee were two of the young men who had been so excited by the fancy car, including the one with the black base-ball cap and the knife. They reminded Diego of the young men in his father's prison, with more confidence than sense, always needing to prove their manhood.

"Meet Dario and Leon," Bonita said, sound-ing as impressed with them as Diego was.

Dario and Leon weren't sure whether to be insulted that their teammates were kids, or excit-ed because it gave them a chance to act like big men. It was comical watching them trying to sort it out. Diego caught Bonita's eyes and saw that she was thinking the same thing.

Deborah Ellis

"The first thing we all need," Dario said, "are battle names." Dario was the guy in the baseball cap.

Diego bit his lip to keep from laughing, but Bonita boldly asked, "Why?"

"So we'll know what to call each other."

"Why don't we just use our real names?"

"You're too young to understand," Dario told her. "Trust me on this. I'm going to go by the name Wolf."

"I thought I was Wolf," Leon said. "I thought of it. You wanted Spear."

"I'm Wolf," declared Dario loudly, "and Leon will be called Spear."

"You got the better name," whined the Spear. "A spear needs someone to throw it. A wolf acts alone."

"Wolves hunt in packs," Diego said.

Dario looked crestfallen, then sat up and said, with his finger in Diego's face, "Not lone wolves!"

Diego decided to let it pass.

"And you," Dario said, pointing at Diego. "You are as cute as a bug. We will call you Bug."

Diego didn't care, and he didn't really mind.

A bug was small, but it could do a lot of damage, like a mosquito that carried malaria, or the bug that spread chagas.

"Now we need a name for you," Dario said to Bonita.

Diego watched her steely eyes half close in a glare.

"My name is Bonita," she said.

Wolf and Spear wisely left it at that.

"Is there a list?" Bonita asked.

They looked at her blankly.

"A list," she repeated, "of the things we need."

"It's up here," Leon said, tapping his forehead.

"Maybe we should put it someplace more secure," Bonita suggested. "In case something happens to you." She got up, walked to where her family's things were piled against the bridge railing and came back with a pen and a school notebook.

"I will be the keeper of the list," she announced.

"We need paint for the signs," Diego said, while Bonita wrote. "And boards or something to make the signs with. And brushes."

"Lanterns," said Bonita, as she wrote it down.

"Cloth for bandanas," Dario said, eager to get in on it. "Vinegar."

Bonita paused in her writing. "What do we need that for?"

"See? You don't know everything. Write them down."

"Where do we get these things?" Diego asked.

"We scavenge. We ask. We take."

"You mean we steal. I'm not sure everybody would agree." Bonita put her pen down on the pavement.

"Well, all right, we don't steal, but…"

Whatever else Leon was going to say was lost to Diego. Someone was shouting.

"Runner!"

"You take it, Bug," Dario ordered, and Diego was happy to get moving. He could tell he wasn't going to like the meetings part of the blockade.

Others seemed to, though. As he ran from group to group carrying messages, people seemed to be enjoying themselves, talking and debating.

"I don't mind carrying messages," he told Mr.

Ricardo. Diego was carrying the latest slogan suggestions from the sign-painting committee to the communications committee. "But why don't they get up and do it themselves?"

"This is a drill," Mr. Ricardo said. He was on his way into the forest to help dig latrines. "We're practicing for when that won't be possible, for when we all have to stay at our posts. The committees are practicing talking to each other this way, and you are practicing carrying messages."

That made some sense to Diego, although he didn't really understand.

"At the same time," Mr. Ricardo continued, "you're getting to know names and faces, and what people's responsibilities are. As a runner you'll know the whole picture of the blockade better than most of us. That's a very powerful job."

Diego liked the sound of that. "I guess I'd better get back to it, then."

Later that day, leaving Bonita on the bridge to run messages, Diego, Dario and Leon, along with a few volunteers from other committees, went into the village to the north. They took a shortcut through the jungle so they didn't have

Deborah Ellis

to go up the hill and around the canyon the way the highway did.

"We'll need to block off the trail," someone said. "Or at least hide it. We don't want strangers, or the army, coming through here and surprising us."

Diego looked out across the gorge. He could see the bridge. "Why don't we post a lookout at the side of the bridge to watch the trail? It would work in the daytime, anyway."

"Good idea," some of the others said. "Tell the security committee when we get back."

"What about camouflage?" Dario asked, walking behind Diego. "In the army they teach you to blend in with the jungle and lie very still so that you look like a rock, and then when your enemy is all relaxed and doesn't suspect — Pow!" He gave Diego a swat across the top of his head on the word "Pow."

Diego kept his mouth shut. He knew all about guys like Dario. They might be on the same side, but that didn't mean much.

The trail opened up at the side of the highway. Cars and trucks lined the road, abandoned, motors shut off.

"Everybody's at the chicheria," Leon said.

The little village, with its church, school, few shops and scattered eateries, seemed extra full for a day that wasn't a market day. People weren't doing much, though. Just sitting, walking slowly from one place to another, looking at their watches. More vehicles were parked anywhere there was room.

"They're waiting for the blockade to lift," Diego realized. He saw the bus with its door open, some people still inside, sleeping with their faces flattened against the windows. He saw the trucks full of lumber and cattle.

"Will those cows get fed?" he asked. "Will they get water?"

"Why do you care?" Dario asked. "You should be asking, 'Will we get fed? Will we get water?'"

"Will we get chicha?" asked Leon. He and Dario started toward one of the taverns, but were pulled back by their friends.

"You want people to know we're from the blockade?" their friends asked. "Let's just get what we need and get out of here."

The group went from house to house, shop to

Deborah Ellis

shop. They kept to the back streets as much as possible. For now the people being kept waiting were drunk on chicha and sun, but tempers could fly at any moment.

The cocaleros had friends in the village. They also spent their money there, when they had any. In some ways the villagers were as dependent on the coca crop as the cocaleros. Cocaleros with no money meant shops without customers.

The bundles grew in Diego's arms. People helped out with what they could. An old bed sheet to turn into a banner. Tins with small amounts of paint left. A stained tablecloth to be cut into bandanas. Plastic buckets for water.

The protesters made their requests quietly, not wanting to arouse the suspicions of the folks who were stuck in the village because of the blockade. We won't be hard to spot, Diego thought. We're the only ones carrying things. Everyone else was taking their siestas, or pacing impatiently.

"Candles," someone said when they were standing behind the church. "Someone should ask the priest for candles."

"Send the Bug," Dario ordered. "He looks angelic. Don't blow it, Bug."

Diego handed the things he was carrying to one of the others. "Don't leave without me," he said. "I don't know if I can find the trail without you."

"Move, don't talk," said Dario.

Diego went around to the front doors of the old stone church. He opened the heavy wooden door. Inside the light was dim, coming through the stained glass in easy streams. The air was cool and smelled of incense and candle wax.

Diego walked slowly up the aisle, wondering where the priest was. He liked the coziness of the little church. The cathedral in Cochabamba, where he sometimes went to light a candle for one of the old prisoners, was grand and fancy. The God who went there would have too many important things on his mind to listen to the prayers of ordinary people. But in this simple church, Diego thought, maybe prayers could be heard.

A door opened at the side of the altar.

"What do you want?" The priest came into the sanctuary, walking toward Diego. He was an older man, Spanish, not Quechua or Aymara. The soft glow from the candles made the top of

Deborah Ellis

his bald head shine. "Catechism class isn't until tomorrow — and how dare you come into my church looking like that?"

Diego knew he was filthy. He'd been thrown in the dirt, he'd worked in the coca bushes, he'd been busy.

"I'm with the cocalero blockade, Father," he said. "I'm here to ask you for some candles."

The priest crossed the distance between them in a few quick, angry strides.

"You want our holy candles to light up your unholy activity?"

"Unholy?" Diego didn't understand. "People just want their coca back. They just want to put tin roofs on their houses." He was beginning to doubt that this was a place where God would listen.

"You are breaking the law, and I want no part of it," the priest said, leaning in closer. He was a spitter. "You are all going to be arrested!"

Near Diego was a station of the cross, the one where Jesus was being taken away by the Roman soldiers.

"Jesus was arrested," he said.

"Get out!" the priest yelled. "Get out of my church!"

Diego got out. He went around back with empty hands, but the others had left.

"What do I do now?" he asked out loud.

A small door opened at the back of the church. A nun ran out, her hands full of candles.

"Your friends had to rush away," she said, handing him the candles. "A fight might have started with people waiting for the blockade to be lifted. Don't worry. You'll catch up." She told him where to find the trail entrance. "God bless you," she added with a giggle, then ran back into the church.

Baffled, a little scared, but quite suddenly very happy, Diego headed for the trail.

He passed two young gringo men with long hair. They were lying on the ground, heads propped up on their giant backpacks.

"Hey, little brother," they called out as he rushed by. "What's your hurry? Enjoy the day!" Then they laughed.

I am enjoying the day, Diego thought, as he found the entrance to the trail. He put down the candles and dragged bushes and branches across the pathway for camouflage. Then he picked up the candles and headed for the bridge.

Deborah Ellis

CHAPTER EIGHT

Diego stood his first watch on the second night of the blockade, at the south end of the bridge.

The south end, the farthest from the town, was the quietest. Cars weren't lined up at this end. There was another blockade nearly twenty kilometers farther south that was holding them back.

Ahead of Diego was the dark Bolivian night, the thick growth of trees on each side adding shadows and whispers. Behind him the community of the bridge was settled down for the night. They made quiet human noises – whispers and snuffles, snores and coughs. The children's area was set up at the south end. Under the tarp, mothers and little ones were sleeping and dreaming.

It had been a fairly quiet day. A couple of times travelers had tried to break through the blockade on foot. The north barrier was so built up by now that there was no way cars could cross. Two hikers were allowed to go through after they asked respectfully and explained to everyone that they were doing a rainforest study and had the papers to prove it. The education committee nabbed them to give a speech to everyone on Bolivia's ecosystems. Diego only half listened to it. They spoke as though they were used to lecturing people who had to listen to them. Diego suspected they were allowed to go on their way just to shut them up.

A group of cyclists from Spain tried to get through by first walking their bikes on to the bridge, saying they wanted to join the protest. But halfway across they mounted up and tried to ride off. They were promptly turned around. Leon and Dario wanted to add the bicycles to the barriers, but Mrs. Ricardo said simply, "That's not why we are here," and sent the cyclists biking back to the town.

They did have two travelers staying with them now on the bridge – the gringos Diego had passed on his way back from the village. He thought of them as richer, whiter versions of Leon and Dario, except with wild hair and scruffy beards. They had been passengers on the bus that was stuck in town, and decided they wanted to be part of the blockade rather than wait around in the village. They took up a lot of space with their giant backpacks, their rubber sleeping mats and their sleeping bags. They kept burning incense that smelled like burnt strawberries. They played shrill tunes badly on tin flutes, read novels and told each other jokes in English, but Diego never saw them do any work.

Diego sat on an old wooden crate a little apart from the others on watch. They were playing cards by the light of one of the nuns' candles. They'd invited him to join them, but he wanted to watch the darkness.

I'm protecting everybody, he thought. It was a good feeling. He listened to the people noises behind him and looked out into the darkness ahead. It felt good to be doing his job.

Then two hands smacked against Diego's eyes, blinding him from behind.

Diego sprang off his seat, twisting and turning, hot and cold with terror, too scared to scream. He was sure that the monster from his nightmares had crawled out of the quicksand to get him.

"Whoa!" he heard a young man's voice say as the hands came off his eyes. He spun around to see Dario, laughing at Diego's fear. The card players looked up and were laughing, too. "You think there are ghosts out there? Booooo!" Dario raised his arms like a zombie and made an ugly face.

"Quiet down," hissed a woman from underneath the tarped-over area. "Children are sleeping."

Diego used the distraction to pull himself together, pressing his fingernails into the palms of his hands to keep himself from crying.

"Just joking," he said.

"Sure you were." Dario took his place on the crate. "Anything happening out there?"

"It's quiet." He wished Dario would go. He wanted his seat back, and he preferred the quiet night to dumb conversation. But he couldn't ask Dario to leave. Being on a blockade was all about getting along with people. The bridge wasn't big enough for quarrels.

"Vargas wants to see you," Dario said. "I'm supposed to relieve you."

Vargas was the rep from the coca growers' union, the people who had organized the blockade. He'd given a big speech when he arrived just before sunset.

What if Vargas had found out that Diego wasn't a real cocalero, but just a stray prison kid far from home? Would he be kicked off the blockade? Where would he go?

"What does he want?" Diego asked nervously.

"Am I an encyclopedia?" Dario asked. Diego had to admit that Dario was anything but, although he kept that opinion to himself. "Move it, Bug."

Diego headed across the bridge, stepping carefully around cocaleros stretched out on mats and blankets, little groups sitting and talking, mothers soothing their babies back to sleep, old couples holding hands and whispering. Portable grills smoked with the cooling charcoal of the evening meal.

My parents would love it here, Diego thought, as he had nearly every hour since arriving at the blockade.

"Have you seen Vargas?" he asked a man who was leaning against the bridge railing and quietly strumming a very small guitar.

The man nodded toward the north end of the bridge and kept strumming. The notes he played were so light and delicate it was almost as if they were rising up from the river.

Diego saw a group of adults standing together and talking. He couldn't see their faces, but he recognized Vargas's cowboy hat. He'd got it in La Paz, he told them in his speech, from a tourist who couldn't fit it into his luggage.

"I wear it to remind me that Bolivia will one day soon no longer need hand-outs from foreigners. We are rich in resources, and one day we will keep Bolivian resources for Bolivian people, not give them away to rich countries in exchange for trinkets — or John Wayne hats!" Everyone had laughed at that line, particularly when Vargas had raised the hat and waved it in the air.

Diego knew that some adults hated being interrupted by kids, even when it was important. But he had a job to do, so he went right up to them.

"Mr. Vargas? You sent for me?"

The adults laughed – even Vargas – but it was a nice laugh.

"You will swell his head," one of them said. "He will outgrow his hat and have to find another gringo tourist, one with a bigger head."

They all laughed again, but quietly, so they didn't disturb the others.

"Diego, you are doing a fine job here, and we are glad you are with us," Vargas said, putting his hand on Diego's shoulder. "This is the future of Bolivia," he said to the group, "and we are in very good hands."

Diego's chest puffed with pride. He felt like he could fly, or do anything else that came his way.

"Diego, I have another task for you. Will you take it on, along with the work you are already doing?"

"Of course, Mr. Vargas. Anything."

"Please, just call me Vargas. I want you to watch out for my son. I have to leave in the morning to travel to the other blockades in the area, and I'll feel better about leaving him here if I know he has a friend."

Diego groaned a little to himself. The son of

a respected man was likely to be a jerk, someone Diego would prefer to throw off the bridge rather than spend time with.

"He's been ill," Vargas said. "He is not strong, and he'll be safer here than traveling with me. His mother is dead," Vargas added. "There is just the two of us."

"He will be safe with me," Diego said. He couldn't refuse. He just hoped the son wasn't too much of a pain, and anyway, he was used to little kids.

"Thank you, Diego. I knew you were the one to ask. His name is Emilio, and you will find him somewhere on the bridge." Vargas shook Diego's hand with real gratitude, then went back to his discussions with the adults.

Somewhere on the bridge. Diego thought that probably meant under one of the sleeping tarps, where the little kids were forced into sleeping by their parents. There was a lot happening on the blockade, and a lot of people to play with. The little ones were reluctant to go to sleep in case they missed something.

"Is there an Emilio in here?" Diego asked in a whisper, bending low to ask one of the mothers sitting there. She was nursing her baby, and she shook her head.

Diego got the same result when he asked at other sleeping areas. He walked up and down the bridge, looking for a little kid who should have been in bed.

"You look lost," said a boy about his age. He was leaning over a chess board lit up by a candle stuck in an old tin can with the side cut out of it. "It takes a special skill to get lost in the middle of a bridge."

"Do you know a little kid named Emilio?" Diego said. "I'm supposed to look after him. A job directly from Vargas." He was unable to keep the bragging from his voice.

"You play chess?" the boy asked.

"Sure."

"You give me a decent game, and I'll tell you where to find Emilio."

"You don't think I can beat you?"

"I'll be satisfied if your playing doesn't put me to sleep," said the boy, but he said it with a smile.

There had been some good chess players in the men's prison, and Diego had learned a few tricks from them when he visited his father. He and the other boy were evenly matched, playing quickly, their moves speeding up as the game went on. The boy across from him grinned as the speed picked up, and they took off into a sort of chess dance. A ring of blockaders soon surrounded the little bit of light from the candle, watching the boys play.

It ended in a draw.

"Emilio, you play like your father," someone said, patting him on the shoulder. The group broke up, leaving the boys alone.

"Your father is Vargas," Diego said, looking across the chess board at the boy. "Why didn't you tell me?"

"Would it have improved your game?" Emilio asked with a grin.

"You're a good player," Diego admitted. "Did your father teach you?"

"My mother," Emilio said. "She taught us both."

"I'm sorry she's dead," Diego said, then realized it was a very stupid thing to say after just being introduced. "Mine's in prison," he added quickly. "So's my father. He taught me to play."

"Then we're kind of in the same boat," Emilio

said. "I know why you were looking for me. My father worries because I've been sick a lot, but I'm tougher than I look. So if you've got other friends you want to be with instead…"

"I had a friend," Diego said. "His name was Mando. He's dead."

"Well, I'm not going to die any time soon, no matter what my father thinks. Another game?"

They set the chess board up again and played two more games, slower and easier, before they went to sleep. Then they joined a row of others sleeping on blankets spread out on the hard pavement. Diego watched Emilio take an inhaler out of his pocket and put it beside him on the mat.

"There was a kid in my mother's prison who used one of those," Diego said. "She had asthma."

"It just helps me breathe," Emilio said. "I don't really need it."

"Keeps your dad from worrying," Diego said. Emilio nodded, then closed his eyes.

It reminded Diego of sleeping beside Mando in the jungle, in the clearing by the coca pit. He ached for his friend. It took him a long time to get to sleep.

CHAPTER NINE

Diego, Bonita and Emilio were on livestock detail.

People came and went from the blockade during the day, going along forest trails to their homes to check that all was well, then returning with things they could spare. Before long, the protesters were well organized.

"Please check with the runners committee before you go back to your homes," Vargas had announced at a morning meeting before he left to visit another blockade. "Let us each contribute what we can so that we can all have what we need."

Dario and Leon were good at scrounging — especially old tires, which they piled up at both ends of the bridge, although Diego couldn't imagine why. They even found an old wrecked rowboat and organized a gang of men to drag it up the bank and across the north end of the bridge, bolstering the barrier there. Propped up a bit, it also provided extra shelter. The sign painters were quick to paint slogans on it: *Solidarity!* and *Power to the People!*

Dario and Leon could do the big things, but they weren't so good at getting the smaller day-to-day things people needed to make life possible on the bridge. Bonita happily took over. She took seriously her job as Keeper of the List, a job she was perfectly suited for because it put her in charge. People came to tell her what they needed, and they came to her when an item was found so she could check it off the list and see that it got to where it was meant to go.

"I'm too busy here," she said when her mother suggested she go and look after the animals on the nearby farms. Diego knew she simply didn't want anyone else having control over her list, not even for a little while, not even her mother. But Mrs. Ricardo insisted.

"You need to stretch your legs," Mrs. Ricardo

said. "You need to take a break from the blockade while you can. Go."

Bonita was tough, but her mother was tougher.

Of the three of them, Bonita was the only one from the area. It put her in a better mood that she held all the information. It cheered her up even more when she learned that Emilio hadn't lived on a farm since he was a small child.

"We live in Cochabamba," he said. "We moved there after my mother died. My father works in the union office. We share a room in a boarding house."

Diego wanted to find out more, but he knew instinctively that he and Emilio talking about something that Bonita didn't know about would just put her back into a bad mood, and he didn't want anything to spoil the day.

A labyrinth of footpaths crisscrossed the whole area, and Bonita knew them all. Diego and Emilio had to move fast to keep up with her.

Emilio started breathing hard and had to stop.

"What's the hurry?" Diego shouted to Bonita.

"You think I can't keep up?" Emilio asked. "I'm faster than you are." He took a breath of his inhaler, then pushed by Diego to catch up with Bonita.

They had a list of farms to visit and a list of chores to do at each one. They had to hunt around for chicken feed, and there were many pails of water to fetch. The farms were pretty much all the same – some a little less poor than others, but not by much. They all had small mud and stone houses in better or worse states of repair, a few chickens, a vegetable garden and a field of ripped-out coca bushes.

"The kids at this farm haven't had shoes in a year," Bonita said when they arrived at the third ruined farm. "They come to school barefoot and they're always getting sick. They never have pencils or anything. They just sit in class stinking because they don't have soap or a change of clothes. Their coca money would have made such a difference."

They pulled up a few weeds from the potato patch, but there wasn't much they could do to make that farm look better.

The Ricardo farm was the last on their list. It

was the first time Diego had seen it since the day the helicopter came. It looked bare and forlorn without the coca bushes.

Bonita started to cry. Then she swatted Diego across his chest to try to cover up.

"Come meet the llama," Diego told Emilio, to give Bonita some privacy and so she wouldn't hit him again. "He hates everybody."

"Sounds like some people I know," said Emilio, following Diego to the paddock. They cleaned the llama and donkey pens, put in fresh straw, feed and water. They spent a lot of time petting and talking to the donkey.

"When my parents get out of prison, we'll become farmers again," Diego said, letting the donkey chew on his shirt.

"I like cement," Emilio said. "I'm a city kid now. I like lights and traffic and noise and things happening. What prison are your parents in?"

"San Sebastian. Two prisons on one square."

"Is that near the amusement park?" Emilio asked. "I was there once on a school outing. The rides are fun. You ever go on the Rounder?"

"No," Diego said. They barely had money to eat. There was certainly no money for rides.

"You'll love it. It will make you throw up. My father works in construction when the union doesn't have money to pay him, which is usual."

"I hope you two are enjoying your holiday," Bonita called out. "I'm glad there are at least two people in this world who don't have any work to do."

"I guess she's feeling better," Diego said. They gave the donkey a final pat, steered clear of the llama and fetched water for the vegetable garden.

They all went for a quick swim before heading back to the blockade. Bonita brought a bit of soap from the house and they were able to get clean.

"Don't use too much," she ordered, when she saw Emilio running the bar through the mop of curls on his head. "I want to take it to the blockade."

Emilio gave his head a couple of more rubs with the soap, then placed the bar on a leaf at the edge of the river where it could dry.

The cold water gave Diego new energy. He was eager to get back to the bridge. They had their arms full of vegetables and blankets, and Bonita carried a sack that squeaked and moved.

"Your pen works well," she said.

"Our pen," Diego said. "We did it together."

Bonita didn't argue.

The pathway she led them on opened up on top of the hill overlooking the bridge. They sat for a moment and looked down at the blockade.

There were cookfires in the dirt at the side of the road, built there so the flames wouldn't ruin the pavement. "It's our pavement," someone had explained to Diego. "Why would we ruin what's ours?" Someone was playing a singing game with the little ones. Their voices traveled up the hill. All over the bridge he could see people meeting, working and resting up for what was to come.

"My father says the whole country is shut down," Emilio told them. "There are blockades all over. Nothing is moving."

Diego put his finger on the ground in front of a caterpillar, and it crawled on to his hand.

"There must be a lot of angry cocaleros in Bolivia," he said.

"Not just cocaleros," Emilio said. "Teachers, miners, people like Dario and Leon who work on other people's farms. Lots of people. My

110   *Deborah Ellis*

father says some prisoners are even going on hunger strikes to support the protests."

Diego didn't like thinking of his mother and father going hungry, not even for a good reason. Mama would never let his little sister Corina go hungry, though. She'd find some way to feed her.

"My father can travel across the barricades because he's with the union," Emilio said. "But I'm afraid the army or the police will stop him and arrest him on the way, and I'd never know." He let the caterpillar crawl from Diego's hand on to his.

At least I know where my parents are, Diego thought. It would be awful to not know.

Bonita's turn with the caterpillar came next. She let it crawl over the bare skin on her lower arm.

"How long will this go on?" she asked Emilio.

"The water protests in Cochabamba went on for weeks," Emilio said.

"We were locked in at the prison," Diego remembered. "I had to stay inside. I hated it." Food was short, electricity was off, guards had to work extra shifts because their replacements couldn't get in to work, and that made them more foul than usual.

"It started just like this," Emilio went on. "We put up barricades, got ourselves organized, and everybody worked together. It felt like a party at the beginning. Then the police came, we made them back down, and everything felt like a victory."

Diego plucked a strand of long grass from the ground and started to pull it apart. It was the sort of grass Mrs. Ricardo turned into baskets.

"And then what happened?" he asked.

"Then it got nasty."

It was time to get back. The children stood up, dusted the dirt and grass from their clothes and picked up their bundles.

"My father is so brave," Emilio said as they started walking. "He's so strong. I wish I wasn't so weak."

"You'll do," said Bonita, pushing past him and leading the way back down the hill.

"That's probably the nicest thing she's ever said to anybody," Diego told Emilio. Then they had to run to keep up. Bonita liked to move fast.

CHAPTER TEN

"Scared?"

Bonita had something on Diego, more than she usually had, and she was enjoying it.

"Bet you can't do it," she said.

"Of course I can," Diego said. "I've done it a hundred times."

"Sure you have. Go ahead. Show me. Maybe I can learn something from you." Bonita handed him the knife and the squealing guinea pig she'd taken from her sack.

Diego looked to Emilio and Martino for help, but they just grinned and settled down to watch on a rock by the side of the road.

The guinea pig was not used to being held. It squirmed and wriggled and peed all over Diego's hand. Diego stuck the knife handle between his teeth so he could get a better grasp of the little creature. He finally got what he thought was a solid grip on it with both hands.

Then Martino said, "How are you going to do it? You need another hand for the knife."

Diego tried clutching the animal against his chest, but it tucked its little face into his shirt.

By now Bonita, Emilio and Martino were falling over themselves laughing.

"Come on, Diego," Bonita said. "There are hungry people here waiting to be fed."

Diego finally admitted defeat. He handed the knife and the animal back to Bonita. He couldn't watch while she made one quick cut across the guinea pig's throat. In an instant it was over. She held the carcass over a pail so the blood would drain away. Another cut, straight down the belly, and the guts tumbled out into the bucket. Within moments she had the guinea pig skinned and skewered and ready to roast on the fire.

"Seven more to go," she said. The other guinea pigs in the pen were still too young to eat.

Deborah Ellis

Diego and Emilio left her to it and went looking for another chore to do. Any task would be better than that one, Diego thought.

There was a feast that evening. Candles and oil lanterns lit up the bridge. The little ones were allowed to stay up as late as they could manage, falling asleep among the dancers and in the laps of their mothers or fathers.

"It's good to celebrate now while we can," Mrs. Ricardo said. "Who knows what will happen tomorrow? Come, Diego. Dance with me."

Diego had never danced before, but it was dark enough that he figured no one would see him. Besides, how could he refuse Mrs. Ricardo? He skipped and hopped and enjoyed feeling like a fool, breathing in the clean Bolivian air, surrounded by his new family and friends. The sound of zamponas, of charangos and drums was joined by clapping and foot stomping.

Diego laughed and laughed. He felt free and happy. It was a fine, fine night. He feasted on roasted rabbit and guinea pig — which tasted a lot like the rabbit — and empanadas and bananas. When he got tired of eating and dancing, he joined Emilio, who was playing one of the drums. Emilio made room on the log and they pounded away into the night.

Bonita was standing watch at the south end. Diego took her a plate of food and sat down beside her.

"Thank you," she said, which surprised him, but he let it pass.

"I ate one of your guinea pigs," he said, "or part of one. It was good."

"That's not the only way to prepare them," she said. "Mama has this way she cooks them for special days like Christmas or Easter. She boils them first, takes the skin off, puts them in salt for a few hours, then fries them with a chili peanut sauce she makes. That's the best way, but roasting is easiest for a big crowd."

It was the most she'd ever said to him without sneering.

"Well, everybody seemed to like them," Diego said. "Ever think of raising them for money?"

"We trade some for rice," Bonita said. "We don't grow rice." He already knew that.

"People sell them in the market in Cochabamba," Diego said. "Big sacks full.

Maybe you could raise enough to sell, maybe make enough money for school."

Bonita stopped eating and stared at him. He was afraid for a moment that the old Bonita had returned, but she just said, "There's no more room under our stove."

"Maybe," Diego started, a plan taking shape in the notebook in his mind, "maybe we could build them a separate little house attached to the wall by the stove, so they'd get warmth from the fire but would have more room to grow. Maybe you could raise forty or fifty all at once."

Bonita chewed thoughtfully on a potato.

"You talk as if you're not leaving," she said. "You talk as if you plan on staying here. Maybe you think you'll just keep living on our farm."

Diego didn't know what to say, although there was some truth in Bonita's words. He knew he needed to see his family, he needed to make things right, but he didn't know whether he could live in the prison again without going crazy. He'd begun to daydream of having enough money to travel back and forth, to support his family, but also to spend most of his time with the Ricardos. He'd even started to think about bringing Corina back with him. Mrs. Ricardo would take good care of her, and farm work and space to play would take the whine out of her.

"It's not your farm," she said. "I'm the oldest. That should count for something, even though I'm a girl. I do as much work on the farm as a boy would do. Twice as much."

Diego had a feeling the conversation had switched into something else, but he wasn't sure what. Then Bonita switched it back to him.

"I'm glad that we helped you out when you needed it, but now there are a lot of other families you can turn to. We didn't have enough to go around before they stole our coca. Don't think you're moving in."

"I'm not. I don't!"

"You don't even need to stay on the blockade, do you? You're not really one of us. You don't need to stay."

It was a mean thing to say. Diego didn't even bother to ask her why she said it. He just got up off the log and walked away.

He walked through the party to the north end of the bridge, as far away from Bonita as he could get without leaving the blockade. He leaned against one of the tree branches that made up part of the barrier.

"What's the matter, Bug?" Dario was there, drinking chicha with his buddies. "Girl troubles? They only get worse, my friend, but oh, is it worth it!"

Dario started to brag. From Diego's experience, the more bragging, the less there was to tell. He turned his ears off and stared out from the north end of the bridge, then found Emilio for a few games of chess.

His mind wasn't on the game, though, and Emilio beat him easily, twice.

"Go to bed," Emilio said. "I'd rather play with Santo."

CHAPTER ELEVEN

"Good morning, campesinos!"

A woman's voice boomed out from a megaphone, making Diego jump right out of his sleep.

A couple of the little kids started to cry at being woken up suddenly. That didn't stop the old woman holding the megaphone.

Diego propped himself up on his elbows and nudged Emilio, who was sleeping beside him. They watched the old woman move closer and closer to where Dario, Leon and the other men of the chicha party were sprawled together on a mat, moaning and groaning about the loud noise.

"We are here for a purpose," the old woman announced, the megaphone making the sound of her voice echo down the river. "Some of you seem to think that purpose is to drink chicha. Maybe we should have a meeting to see if everybody feels that way."

Anybody could call a meeting at any time about anything that was bothering them. You didn't have to be a union official. Even Martino called a meeting one afternoon to complain that the young men kept borrowing the children's ball to play soccer on the bridge but wouldn't let the little kids join in. The meeting decided that the young men had to get their own ball or play only under the direction of the little kids.

"I am calling a meeting this morning, right now, to discuss the banning of chicha from the blockade," the old woman continued.

Diego was all in favor of banning the homemade corn beer. He didn't like the taste anyway, and it might mean Dario and Leon would do more work instead of just giving orders.

It was a good-natured meeting. Those with the morning-after heads grumbled, but they were clearly outnumbered.

"Let's put it to a vote, then," Mrs. Ricardo said. "All those in favor of banning the drinking of chicha — and any other alcohol — on the block-ade..."

"Someone's coming!" came a yell from the north end of the bridge.

It wasn't just someone. It was a whole lot of someones. Down the highway came a big group of people armed with sticks, and they were heading toward the blockade.

The protesters scrambled into action. The young children and old people ducked under a tarp in the center of the bridge. Everyone else went to the barricades.

The little kids Martino's age had been given the job of collecting stones, and now Diego saw what they were for, as protesters picked them up, ready to throw.

"Wait until they come close enough!" someone shouted.

"Who are they?" Diego asked.

"Probably the people we turned back on the bus," the man next to him said. "The food and beer have probably run out at the village, and now they think they have a right to come through here."

Diego picked up a stone.

"Get ready," said the man. The crowd was coming closer. "Wait." Diego felt his muscles tense up, and then, "Now!"

Diego threw as hard as he could – not aiming, just throwing. There was yelling all around. Some of the people picked up the stones as they landed and threw them back at the cocaleros. Others got right up to the barricade and started to dismantle it.

"Get them!" the man beside Diego yelled, and they hurled their stones at the barricade busters until they backed away.

Some of the stones landed on people, and Diego saw protesters with blood running down their faces. The medical team hustled them off to the side to be bandaged.

A few of the men managed to make it across the first barricade and were hitting out at the protesters with metal pipes and baseball bats.

"All together!" Diego yelled at Bonita and Emilio and the other kids their age. They swarmed the two men, taking them by surprise and knocking them down to the pavement. Diego and the others kicked at them until one of the protesters pulled them off.

"Let them go," they were told.

"You're all crazy!" the pipe-man yelled. "Let's get out of here. They're all crazy!"

The blockaders kept up the rain of stones until all the people on the highway retreated back up the hill and around the bend to the town, and the clearing became quiet again.

"Did you really think you could break us?" Dario shouted. He leaned against the barricade next to Diego, sweaty and bloody, a black eye already starting to swell and discolor his face. "Did you really think we'd be afraid of you?"

He kept yelling and hooting until Diego's tugs on his arm finally calmed him down.

"You're bleeding," Diego said. "You need the medical committee."

"I'm fine." Dario pulled his arm away. "They didn't hurt me."

But he allowed Diego to take him to the south end of the bridge where the medical team was giving out bandages and cups of hot coca tea.

"Maybe we should sneak into town and blow up a few of their cars," Dario said.

"Maybe you should drink your tea and not

talk like a fool," said a woman on the medical committee.

All over the bridge, people were gathering in committees, discussing what had just happened and what they needed to do next.

There was everything to do. Diego zoomed through the day at top speed, gathering food from the farms, hauling water up from the river, helping to reinforce the barricades, and gathering more and more stones.

"They'll be back," someone said, and they were, later that day.

The battles raged off and on all day long. Watches were doubled on the barricades and switched every two hours so that everyone would have fresh eyes. People ate standing up and on the run.

One of the protesters had a radio that didn't need batteries. He just cranked the handle and it played.

"The cities are running out of food," he announced after listening to the news report. "All of Bolivia is shut down. The government will have to act soon. We'd better be ready."

Diego didn't know how much more ready

they could be. He gathered stones, helped build up their store of food, helped the medical committee cut up bedsheets for bandages and helped the security committee cut up other old cloth for bandanas, tying one around his own neck, even though he didn't really know what it was for.

Someone suggested the women and children leave. It was a suggestion the women ignored.

The day drew to a close, with the sky shifting from evening glow to starry darkness just like every other day. Everyone settled in, tense, and got each other through the night.

CHAPTER TWELVE

Diego and Emilio were on watch at the north end of the bridge when they spotted a lone figure walking toward them down the hill in the middle of the highway.

Emilio gave three short blasts on the whistle that hung around his neck – a gift from one of the little kids on the blockade. Diego ran back to report to the security committee, and to tell Bonita to run to the south end with the information. After so many days on the blockade, they had their procedures down pat.

Diego ran back to Emilio, and they were soon joined by others.

The lone man was getting closer. He walked with his arms out from his sides, and his fingers spread wide to show he wasn't carrying a weapon. He raised one arm in a wave.

"It's the captain," Diego said.

"Pass the word," someone said, and Diego started running again.

A lot of the protesters were gathered by the north barricade by the time Diego got back there. They all wanted to hear what the captain had to say.

"Is someone in charge here?" the captain asked.

"We're all in charge," Mr. Ricardo called back. "We're all cocaleros. We all had our crops stolen, and we all choose to be here."

"Then I will talk with all of you," the captain said. "I am here to ask you to reconsider what you are doing. I am here to show you my willingness to talk."

"Are you willing to give us back our coca?" someone shouted. "Are you willing to leave us alone to run our farms?"

"You can't stay on the bridge forever," the captain said. "You know the government won't allow the highways to remain shut."

"We don't want to stay here forever," Mrs. Ricardo called out. "We only want to stay until we get our coca back. You took it from us, you can return it."

"You know I can't do that," the captain said. He spotted Diego sitting on one of the logs at the side of the barricade and gave him a nod.

"Is everything all right, Diego? Is there anything you need?"

"What do you care?" Diego asked. "You were going to shoot us."

"Well, let me know if you need anything," the captain said.

"We take care of each other," Diego told him.

The captain spoke again to the whole crowd. "We are not enemies. We are all Bolivian. I am of Aymara blood. Most of my men are Aymara or Quechua. We are the working people, just like you are. We can work together to find a solution to this."

"What we want is justice," another woman said. "You seem like a good man, but you cannot give us what we want. We both have our jobs to do. Our job is to fight for our rights. Yours is to threaten people who are no threat to you."

"For now I am in charge of the army here," the captain said, "but I have to answer to my superiors. If they are not happy with me, they will put someone else in charge and bring in soldiers who are not from here, who have no connection to you and who will not care about you. Please keep that in mind and help me find a solution."

"You say that we are not enemies," Mr. Ricardo said. "We extend to you our friendship and say that you are welcome to put down your guns and join our blockade at any time."

After the captain left, there were no more attacks by travelers. Everything was quiet.

This was the first day on the blockade that seemed long to Diego. Emilio was feeling tired and weak, and he slept on and off. He was able to play a bit of chess when he woke up, but weakness would overtake him again in the middle of a game and he would have to lie down.

Diego left the bridge briefly to join groups foraging for firewood, and to join another rocksnake from the river, but for most of the day, time just dragged.

People on the bridge started to annoy him for stupid reasons, and he knew the reasons were stupid. Why should it matter to him if Leon lifted stones as if they were barbells and then felt his arm muscles to see if they'd grown? Why should he care if the guy with the wind-up radio wouldn't find one station and then leave it there, instead of flipping around and around the dial? And he should be grateful that the two gringo backpackers had joined them in the blockade, even with their annoying habits, including playing a game they called hackysack and making horrible noises on their little tin flutes. They spoke in bad Spanish about how their parents back in Chicago would have a fit if they found out that this was where they were spending their vacation, and they kept asking if there was anywhere they could check their email. Diego wanted to throw them off the bridge.

"What's the matter with you?" Bonita asked him as the sun was going down. She joined him as he sat with his back against the railing of the bridge. "You've been grouchy all day."

"Don't act like you care," responded Diego.

"I'm not. I don't."

They looked across the lanes of the bridge to where the two annoying gringos were playing a game of cards while the little kids looked on.

"They have food in their packs," Bonita said. "I saw it. They think their food belongs to them, and they think that our food belongs to them. They eat and they don't share."

"They're on *holiday*," Diego said with a sneer.

"Well, I wish they'd holiday somewhere else. If anything bad happens here, they'll just make it worse."

"They'll be in the way."

"They won't just be in the way," Bonita said. "If anything happens to them, the world will come crashing down on us. A bunch of Bolivians can get hurt or killed, who cares, but let one gringo get a scratch or hurt his toe, and the blame will fall on us."

"Maybe Vargas can ask them to leave when he gets back."

"He only sees the best in people."

"You ask, then," Diego suggested. "You have no trouble seeing the worst."

"I'm sorry for what I said," Bonita told him, "about you not belonging here. It's not true, and I shouldn't have said it."

"It's partly true," Diego said. "I've been thinking of leaving. I need to earn money, and I need to get home."

"So go, then. No one will stop you."

It was a simple statement, but it made Diego feel very lonely, as though no one would care enough to stop him from leaving.

"Let's get rid of them," Bonita said, standing up and glaring at the gringos. "They either help with food and chores, or they get lost."

Surprised and happy to be included in her plan, Diego got up and together they started to cross the lanes of the bridge.

A low rumbling sound made them stop and listen. It got louder. All over the bridge, people stood up and looked around, trying to see what was causing the noise.

Diego saw lights before he saw anything else. Bright beams cast strange shadows on the bridge and forced him to shield his eyes. He was able to make out the shape of a tank.

At the same moment, he heard the *slap-slap* of propellers, and a helicopter rose up from the river bed, shining another spotlight down on the protesters.

The army had arrived.

CHAPTER THIRTEEN

The lights stayed on all night, and the helicopter never really went away. The noise and wind from the propellers terrified the little ones. Nobody was able to sleep. All the shelters they had constructed with their blankets and tarps and any supplies that weren't weighted down flew up and away.

Diego spent most of the night right up against the north barricade. The army lights made the bridge look as bright as day. He passed the hours breathing in diesel fumes and trying to help where he could.

One of the gringo backpackers lost his lucky hat in the river, and he wailed as if he'd lost a child. His buddy calmed him down, and they picked up their packs to go. They shoved past Diego on the north barricade, but were met by the army.

"We need to pass," the gringo who'd lost his cap shouted. "Americanos! We're Americanos!"

"This end is closed. Leave by the other end."

"But our bus is at *this* end, in the village. You have to let us through. We're Americans! This has nothing to do with us!"

Diego would have found it funny if they weren't so annoying. The army refused to let them pass, and they had to go back to the bridge.

"We're calling our embassy!" they screamed.

"Next time we're going to Australia," one of them shouted at the other. "I told you we should have gone to Australia!"

"Share your food," Bonita said, stepping out in front of them. "We've shared with you. If you want to stay here, you have to share with us. Otherwise keep walking off the south end of the bridge."

Diego couldn't stay to watch the outcome of the confrontation – someone was yelling for a runner – but the gringos were no match for Bonita.

The army didn't try to move on to the bridge that night. They stayed outside the barricade, lights on, helicopter hovering above.

All night long the air stank of tank diesel and helicopter fuel. The little village they'd set up was being polluted by sights, sounds and smells that Diego hated.

"Why don't they attack?" Diego asked.

"They're trying to show us how much stronger they are," Bonita guessed. "They're trying to make us afraid."

"Well, it's not working," Leon said, even though his hands were shaking as he untied and retied his bandana.

At dawn the lights were turned off and the helicopter moved away. The captain's voice came over a loudspeaker.

"This is a message for everyone on the bridge. You have made your point. All of Bolivia is listening. With your bravery and your dedication you have shut down the country — you and other blockades like yours. You can claim victory, and I for one will happily concede that you are right."

At the word victory, a cheer went up from the

Deborah Ellis

cocaleros. Diego didn't cheer, though. Victory meant getting their coca back and Diego getting money to go home. The captain wasn't saying anything about that.

"Now I have to tell you something that is bad news for many of you, and it is also bad news for me," the captain continued. "The other blockades in this area have been broken. Some protesters have been injured. It is only a matter of time before I am ordered to do the same thing here, and if I refuse, I will be replaced by someone who will do as they are told. You all know that what I am saying to you is true."

Jeers and boos rose from the crowd on the bridge. The captain waited until the noise had died down again before he went on. "Now is the time for us to act together for the good of Bolivia. We are a nation of many people. Bolivians are not only coca growers. They have many jobs, and they need to get to work. So I am asking you, as a gesture of good faith, to lift your blockade."

This was met with chants of "Justice! Justice! Justice!"

The chants went on for a good long while.

For Diego, screaming out "Justice!" made him feel like he was at least doing something to fight against the tanks and guns that were pointed at them. He shouted and punched his fist in the air.

When the chants had died down a bit, the voice of the captain came over the loudspeaker again.

"You do not have to abandon your blockade altogether. I am asking you for a small gesture only. Lift your blockade for twelve hours. Allow the back-up of traffic to move through so goods can get to market and your fellow citizens can get to where they need to go."

The answer was a resounding "No!"

"Six hours, then," the captain pleaded. "I am being pressured. Lift your blockade for just six hours. Or four hours!"

The "No!" rose up again, but not as loudly as before.

"We should discuss it," someone shouted. "If we want concessions from them, we should be prepared to give something from us."

"They've already taken our coca," shouted a reply. "What more should we give them?"

"We cannot show weakness now that we are winning!" someone else yelled.

"It does not show weakness to discuss something," Mrs. Ricardo said, which made sense to Diego, even though he didn't know how he felt about lifting the blockade. Keeping it or lifting it, neither seemed likely to result in money in his pocket.

The protesters made a crude circle in the middle of the bridge, sitting so everyone could see everyone else. They left just a few people on watch at either end. Diego sat beside Emilio, who was feeling a little better after so much sleep the day before. Diego saw the two gringo backpackers heading off the bridge at the south end. He was sure their packs had been emptied of food by Bonita.

Moments later, he saw Bonita giving away granola bars, biscuits and the other packaged American food the gringos had been hoarding.

The helicopter moved completely away, and the tanks and military trucks shut off their motors. There was quiet in the clearing, and people could hear each other talk.

"Why should we trust them?" someone

asked. "If we lift our blockade, they could prevent us from setting it up again."

"We could set up another blockade somewhere else on the highway," someone else pointed out. "It doesn't have to be here. They can't keep us off all the highways."

"If we do this for them, they might help us with something we need."

"We don't need them to do anything except return our coca and leave us alone."

The discussion went on and on. Some people were used to speaking about such things in front of a large group, and they quickly got to the point. Others took longer to form their thoughts into words. Some just liked to hear themselves talk.

"Are you feeling all right?" Diego asked Emilio, who was leaning against him a little.

"Just tired," Emilio said. "It's nothing." He was breathing a little hard.

"Why don't you use your inhaler?" Diego asked him.

"Why don't you mind your own business?" Emilio said, pushing himself away.

Diego went after him. "Don't be mad. I told your father I'd watch out for you, that's all."

Emilio started to shake him off again, then stopped.

"I lost my inhaler," he said quietly, so no one else around them would hear. "When the helicopters came. All that wind they stirred up."

"Can't you get another one?"

"Sure, I'll just go into the forest and pick one off a tree," Emilio said, then, "They're really expensive."

Money again, thought Diego.

"Don't tell anyone," Emilio pleaded. "They'll make me leave the blockade. Everyone watches out for Vargas's little boy." He spoke the last words with scorn. "They all think I'm weak."

"No one thinks that," Diego said. "I'll look for your inhaler. No one will know."

"No one will know what, Bug?"

Dario and Leon bumped into the boys from behind.

"No one will know that we hate all these meetings and speeches," Diego said.

"I'm with you on that, little Bug," Dario said, putting his arms around Diego's and Emilio's shoulders.

"But Wolf and I have a plan," Leon said,

steering them all to a bit of the bridge away from the others.

"All this talk is starting to bug us, Bug," Dario said, taking off his baseball cap to scratch a mosquito bite on his forehead. "We need to attack."

"We have a plan," Leon said again. "It's a good plan. It will make them take us seriously."

"I've had it with this waiting around for justice. Why should we wait?" Dario asked. "We're going out and taking what is ours."

"We have work to do," Diego said, tugging Emilio by the arm.

Emilio shrugged him off. "What's your plan?"

"We sneak up on them," Leon said. "Take them by surprise."

"We're leaving." Diego pulled Emilio away. Emilio tried to free his arm, but Diego kept pulling.

"Maybe we should listen to them," Emilio said.

"They have nothing to say." Diego had known too many young men like that in his father's prison, full of bold plans to escape, or to make big money, or to become king of the

prison. Their plans always ended up with someone else getting hurt.

"What do you know?" Emilio said. "You've
never been in a demonstration before. You don't
know anything."

"Your father told me to look after you, so —"

Diego was interrupted by the sounds of
more cheers and chants. Protesters rushed by
them and headed toward the south end of the
bridge.

The boys climbed up on to the railing to see
what was happening.

"It's the folks from the other blockade!"
Emilio shouted. "My father is with them! I can
see his hat!"

Emilio dashed away from Diego, then dashed
back to say, "Remember, you promised not to tell
about my inhaler." Then he rushed off to greet
his father.

Diego couldn't watch Emilio and his father
hug each other. It made him miss his own family
too much.

The cocaleros who weren't busy welcoming
Vargas were busy welcoming the new protesters
from the other blockade. The meetings broke up

for awhile as the new people were shown around and information was shared.

Diego heard bits of news as he moved from errand to errand. The army had moved right through the other blockade, using bulldozers and big trucks to knock away logs and rocks. There were a few broken bones from falls and being hit with truncheons. The ones with the bad injuries had stayed behind for medical care, but the ones with the cuts and scrapes had come to this new blockade, wearing their crude bandages with pride.

"We know that the road to justice is not a straight road," Vargas said through the megaphone. "It is a road with bumps and gaps, and it is not a restful road to travel. But we should have no doubt — and those who oppose us should have no doubt — we travel this road together, with joy in our hearts and a vision of a better future stretched out before us."

Diego was suddenly too tired to listen to the speech, and too tired to run any more errands. He sat with his back to the railing and was glad to be unnoticed and unwanted for a little while. He watched without interest as the new blockaders started to have little arguments with the old blockaders. Each group had their own way of doing things. Each group was sure it was right.

"Are you sure you want to leave the cookfire there?" a new protester was saying to the woman who had built and tended the fire for so many days. "The smoke would blow over the bridge less if the fire was on the other side of the road."

"Let me show you how we built up our blockade," one of the new men said to a man Diego knew from the security committee. "I can show you how to make it really strong."

"If you knew how to make it strong, the army wouldn't have run it down," the security committee man said.

Diego leaned his head against the railing and closed his eyes. Around him the noise of voices ebbed and flowed. I should look for that inhaler, he thought. He dozed off in the warm sun.

A loud bang jolted him out of his sleep and on to his feet. He could tell from the stunned looks that the noise had startled the other protesters as well.

For a long moment there was just the shriek-ing of the birds to show that there had been an actual noise, that Diego hadn't dreamed it. Then it happened again — three bangs in a row, like gunshots.

Clouds of smoke rose up from the bridge. All around him Diego heard people coughing and screaming.

"Tear gas!" he heard someone shout. "They're shooting tear gas at us!"

Diego breathed in something painful and poisonous, making him choke, then vomit on to the bridge. He couldn't get any air. Someone dashed up close to him, picked up the gas-spew-ing canister and hurled it back over the north barricade.

"Splash water in your eyes," Leon shouted as he ran by. "Don't rub them, you'll make it worse."

But Diego's eyes were too full of tears for him to be able to find the water. When he got close just by accident, someone tossed the boiled drinking water on to the pavement.

"There's tear gas in the water," a voice said. "It's all contaminated."

"We need more water." He saw a woman hurry past him with two empty pails to get water from the river. "We should have been better prepared for this!"

The truce between the army and the blockade was over. Protesters threw rocks and sticks at the soldiers. Diego heaved a tear-gas canister back across the barricade.

"Don't throw them in the river," Mr. Ricardo urged everyone. "It's our river. Don't poison it."

The air was full of smoke and gas. All the soldiers were wearing gas masks, so the tear gas didn't bother them.

"I need your help, Bug!" Dario grabbed Diego's wrist and ran with him to the south end of the bridge. He pulled two containers of gasoline out from the shade of a tree. "All over the tires," he ordered.

Diego hesitated. He didn't understand what he was being asked to do.

"The smoke will give us cover," Dario shouted, as he splashed gasoline on to the stack of rubber. "They can't see us, they can't shoot us. Leon's doing the north end. Pour!"

Diego poured. When the tin was empty,

Dario pushed him back, lit a match and tossed it on the pile.

Flames rose up in a whoosh. Diego felt the heat on his face.

"Pull your bandana up!" Dario yelled at him. "Come over here!" He picked up a jug of vinegar. "Close your eyes!" He splashed Diego's bandana with a handful of vinegar. "It will help with the gas." Then he splashed vinegar on his own bandana.

The flames from the gasoline burned themselves out, and thick black smoke from the smoldering tires rose up and mixed with the tear gas.

Diego stumbled around the bridge, his eyes stinging and full of tears. He had to stop every few minutes to cough and catch his breath. The vinegar-soaked bandana didn't seem to be doing him any good — maybe he'd put it on too late. He pushed it down around his neck so he could throw up more freely.

He had no idea how much time was passing. He heard gun shots, and helicopters, and lots of angry shouting. The noise was deafening. Children screamed from fear and from the gas.

148 *Deborah Ellis*

"We have to remove the babies," Mrs. Ricardo said, running down the bridge with a wailing Santo in her arms. "We have to get them up high, away from the gas."

"I know a place," Diego yelled. He took Santo, who pulled Diego's hair and screeched in terror. Mrs. Ricardo spotted Martino trying to throw rocks, even though he was crying from the gas. She grabbed him, and Diego led them all to the bottom of the trail that led up to the ridge where he had sat with Bonita and Emilio after livestock duty.

"Up there," he said, pointing.

Mrs. Ricardo took Santo. "Send the others up. And we'll need clean water."

Diego ran back to the bridge. He tried to point old people and folks with little kids to the trail, but there was so much chaos that he couldn't make himself understood.

"Help me get the little ones ones on to the ridge," he yelled at Bonita when he bumped into her. His eyes were watering so badly that he was nearly blind. "Your mother's already there."

"I'll get Emilio to help," she said.

Emilio! In all the chaos, Diego had forgotten about his responsibility. His own chest and throat were on fire. How could Emilio be all right? He didn't have his inhaler! Diego had promised to look for it, but he'd fallen asleep instead.

Arms outstretched in front of him, he collided with person after person.

"Emilio?" he yelled at each one. "Emilio?"

In the end he found his friend by stepping on him. Emilio was on the pavement, his head half-buried under a tarp to try to escape the gas. Diego bent low over him. Emilio was gasping for breath, like a fish out of water. His skin was frighteningly pale.

Diego tried to drag Emilio away, but he wasn't strong enough. Instead he grabbed hold of something white – a shirt? a towel? – and ran to the north end of the bridge. He climbed the barrier and stood at the top, hopping on to the old rowboat that was propped up there.

Furiously, he waved the white cloth over his head. He did it without discussion, or debate, or the consent of the other protesters.

"Stop firing!" Diego heard. The shooting stopped, and the clearing went quiet, except for

Deborah Ellis

the crying of children and the wounded, and the sounds of vomiting and choking.

The captain took off his gas mask and stepped forward.

"Help my friend," Diego said. "He's on the bridge. He can't breathe."

The captain called for medics. Young army men ran out with a stretcher and a medical kit. They ran to take care of Emilio.

"People are hurt," Diego said to the captain. "You hurt them."

"What did you think was going to happen?" the captain yelled. "With anyone else in charge, it would have been worse. I'm being pressured to clear this bridge!"

Mr. Ricardo was at Diego's side, along with other protesters.

"Vargas and the medics are with Emilio," he said, lifting Diego down from the barrier.

Then he turned to the captain. "You are the only ones inflicting pain," he said. "You have gas and tanks and rubber bullets. We have only our bodies and our willingness to die. You are the ones who must make a choice. You can continue to hurt us, even kill us. Or you can go and tell the government that we will not be scared away!"

With that, and with a squeeze of Diego's shoulder, Mr. Ricardo turned and went back behind the barricade. The others followed him.

Diego let the white cloth of surrender drop through his fingers to the ground, and went to be with his friend.

CHAPTER FOURTEEN

⁕

The bridge became very quiet. The captain ordered all the motors on the tanks and military trucks shut off, and the helicopters stayed away.

"Who started firing tear gas without my orders?" Diego heard him shout. "I wanted to get through this without casualties."

Diego looked back at the bridge from the north barrier. It looked as if a battle had been fought there. Bodies were stretched out on the pavement, hit by flying canisters or debris. He saw red blood through the gray smoke. Blinded with tears and smoke, folks bumped into each other and tripped over each other. There was moaning, and crying, and sounds of anger and pain.

The medics gave Emilio oxygen and medicine. He began to breathe more easily, and the color returned to his cheeks.

"Keep your boy away from tear gas," one of the medics said to Vargas.

"Keep your tear gas away from my boy," Vargas replied. He gathered Emilio into his arms to carry him up to the ridge. His eyes met Diego's for one long moment. Then, with a shake of his head, Vargas took his son to higher ground.

Diego felt very, very tired. Vargas's disappointment was a heavy weight. He leaned against the railing and tried not to feel anything.

"You're the boy who came for the candles," a woman's voice said.

Diego looked up into the face of the nun who had been at the church. His eyes were too teary to see her properly.

"I'm Sister Rosa," she said. "Tilt your head back. This is clean water." Fresh water flowed into Diego's eyes, washing the sting away.

"Actually, it's holy water, from Lourdes," another woman's voice said. "Father Javier brought back big bottles from his last visit to France."

"We think he uses it to try to make his hair

grow back," a third woman's voice said, followed by a blend of giggles.

Sister Rosa patted Diego's face dry with a clean cloth. He was able to see more clearly now.

"Why are you here?"

"Where else should we be?" Sister Rosa smiled at him. "We headed out as soon as we heard the shooting."

"Along the trail," said another nun, going past them to help someone else.

"I guess Father Javier will have to get his own lunch today," said the third, and there were more giggles.

The nuns had clean water and first-aid kits. Diego saw them fan out across the bridge, black veils flapping behind them.

There was a lot to do, and Diego wearily got to it.

The cocaleros decided to move the southern barricade away from the bridge, another fifty meters or so to the south so that they'd have more room now that there were more protesters. The task gave the two blockade groups something to work on together. There was a lot of grumbling from both groups about the smoking tires.

"There was no agreement to do that," protesters said. "Why would we ruin our own air? Why would we ruin our own roads?"

"What did you think the tires were sitting there for?" Dario argued back. "If you didn't want me to burn them, why didn't you say so?"

Diego kept his head down, his mouth shut and did his work, moving branches and logs to the new barrier.

"There are more soldiers down there," someone said, pointing farther south.

Diego put his tree branch with the others and looked down the highway. He saw military trucks and soldiers where the road bent away, but they looked relaxed, talking and smoking.

"They're just waiting," Leon said.

"Waiting for what?"

"Waiting to get us!" Leon said, grabbing Diego as he said it and making Diego wonder why bigger people took such pleasure in trying to scare smaller people.

When he could, he went up to the ridge to be with Emilio.

The ridge was flat and large enough for toddlers to have room to play. Tarps were strung up for shelters, and a cookfire boiled water and cooked pots of chupe. Even protesters who weren't wounded went up there sometimes just to rest on soft ground instead of the hard pavement of the bridge.

Emilio was propped up against a tree trunk. The medicine from the army had helped, but he didn't have his energy back yet. Beside him on an aguayo was a baby he was watching so the parents could be on the bridge.

"I lost the...chess board," Emilio rasped, breathing hard. "Or maybe...the helicopter...blew it away."

"Saves you the pain of a rematch," Diego said, tickling the baby on its tummy.

"My father...says I can't go back to the bridge," Emilio said. "He says I have to stay up here...and rest."

"He's right," said Diego. "You breathed in a lot of gas. Lots of people are up here resting." He waved his arm at the protesters taking advantage of the quiet to catch up on sleep.

"But they can come and go. I've been ordered to stay here. They plopped this...baby down beside me so that I can pretend to be doing something, but all I can do is make my father worry. I'm useless."

Diego could tell from the way Emilio's face winced up that it was painful for him to talk. Diego understood. His own chest and throat still hurt from the gas.

"Looking after a baby isn't useless," he said. "It's the most important thing." He let the baby hold on to his finger and remembered his sister being that small. She had cried a lot. This one wasn't crying. It followed their conversation with big, wide eyes.

"I know...but there are others up here who could do that." Emilio nodded at the older folks around the fire. "My father doesn't think it matters...whether I'm down there or not. He doesn't think I have anything to contribute."

"You whine a lot," Diego said, too fed up to watch his words. "Your father just wants to protect you. Be glad you've got him."

"Leave me alone," Emilio said, folding his arms across his chest and turning his face away.

Someone on the bridge was calling for a runner. Diego got to his feet.

"I'll look for the chess set," he offered.

Deborah Ellis

"Just like you looked for my inhaler?" Emilio asked.

Diego had to walk away.

He lost himself in work, moving his tired and sore body beyond the point of exhaustion.

The piles of stones had to be replenished, and the cocaleros tried to recreate some sort of order on the bridge. They went into the river valley to look for tarps and things the helicopter propellers had sent flying into the wind.

Diego found one of Emilio's chess pieces – a black knight – and brought it to him. He was asleep, with the baby across his lap. Diego put the knight in Emilio's hand and closed his fingers around it. There was no sign of the inhaler.

Clean water had to be hauled up to the bridge, and even higher to the ridge, where it could be boiled and made fit for drinking, out of the range of the tear gas.

Clothes had to be washed, too, to get rid of the gas on them. That meant taking turns wearing blankets while everything was scrubbed with whatever bits of soap could be scrounged. The nuns helped, even rushing back into the village to get more blankets and extra clothes.

People moved slowly, lying and sitting down a lot to rest. Everyone was tired, and their lungs ached. Some had been hit by rubber bullets and limped with big bruises on their legs.

"How's it going, Bug?" Dario asked, sitting down beside Diego on the bridge pavement. "You're a good fighter, you know that?"

"I'd rather be a good farmer," Diego said.

"We fight today so we can farm tomorrow. You want a mint?" He held out two wrapped candies. "Nuns are giving them out. They say it will help our throats."

Diego took one and unwrapped it. He hadn't had a candy in a very long time. It did soothe the pain a bit.

"What do you want to do?" Diego asked suddenly. He realized that he knew almost nothing about Dario in spite of working and living closely with him on the bridge. "In a perfect world, what would you do?"

"In a perfect world?" Dario didn't seem surprised by the question. He looked around in case somebody might be listening, then said in a low voice, "Chickens."

"Chickens?"

Deborah Ellis

Dario explained. "No one in my family has ever owned land. Ever. Go far back in the generations, and we're all mine workers or tenant farmers or workers on the big rubber plantations. I go from farm to farm up here, looking for work, but with the coca crops stolen, no one can hire me. I'm going to have to go to Santa Cruz when this is over, or Cochabamba, and try to get hired on as a day laborer in construction. I've done it before. I hate it. I hate cement.

"In a perfect world, I'd have a small piece of land, with a little house. I'd grow food to eat and to sell, and I'd sit on the porch in the evenings and watch the chickens scratch around in the yard. They would be my chickens on my land — land that would stay in my family forever. It's not too big a dream, to own a little piece of land in the country of my ancestors."

Diego's family had been tenant farmers, too. Someone else was farming their land now, he was sure. Even when his parents got out of prison, there would be no home to go back to.

"What's your dream, Bug?" Dario asked. "In a perfect world?"

"The same as yours," he said.

Sacred Leaf 161

Dario laughed. He took the baseball cap off his own head and put it on Diego's.

"We'll buy land side by side," Dario said. "We'll be neighbors."

For that one moment, Diego could actually see it happening. Then Dario went and ruined the mood by saying, "Spear and I have a plan…"

"Keep me out of it," Diego said, getting back to his feet. "And keep Emilio out of it." He didn't need to add anything about Bonita. She'd keep herself out of it.

"What's the matter, Bug?" Dario called after him. "Too chicken to fight with the big boys?"

He made chicken-clucking sounds. Diego kept walking away. Then he reached up, took off the baseball cap and dropped it to the pavement.

CHAPTER FIFTEEN

Trouble was brewing.

Diego could smell it in the air – something more than the fear and the whiffs of gas and the stench of vomit drying on hot pavement.

He was good at watching people – inmates and guards at the prison, classmates at school, gangs on the street. He was good at smelling trouble.

His father had taught him.

He remembered visiting his father in the men's prison, sitting with him and Mando on the balcony overlooking the courtyard.

"What do you see?" his father would ask. It was sort of a game they played. There wasn't much to do in the men's prison. They would lean against the railing and watch what was going on below.

Sometimes there was a soccer game, but always there was the passing of secrets. "What do you see?" his father would ask, and Diego would whisper, "Two men in the corner planning a fight," or "The man by the woodshop door just stole something."

Diego could almost hear his father now, asking what he was seeing.

He was seeing Leon and Dario making plans. They huddled together and strutted around like they had a big important secret.

He was also seeing protesters starting to bicker. People were tired, they were sore, and they were scared.

"I just want the whole thing to be over," a young woman said to an older one.

"You don't care enough," the older woman accused her. "If people like you were stronger, we would have won already."

It was all nonsense. Diego had seen it in the prison. Inmates attacked each other because they couldn't go after the guards. But it put everybody in a bad mood.

Then the press arrived.

Diego was leaning against the north barricade when the TV crew got into an argument with the army.

"You have no right to keep us away," the reporter said to the captain. "There's still freedom of the press in this country. Or do you want to take that away? Make sure you get his answer on tape," he said to the woman operating the camera.

"I'm not trying to stop freedom of the press," the captain said. "I'm just telling you that we can't guarantee your safety if you go on to the bridge."

"Go get Vargas," Diego was told, but someone had already fetched the union rep and was bringing him to the barricade to talk to the reporters.

Diego kept walking down the bridge. The bickering had stopped. The protesters wanted to present the best picture they could of themselves to the world.

Diego turned his back on the bridge and leaned against the railing, looking down at the river. Sister Rosa was playing with some of the children down there and getting them washed.

"Diego!" Martino called up to him.

Diego decided to join them. He needed a break.

He was soon caught up in some sort of game that had no rules or purpose except to make noise and splash a lot. Sister Rosa didn't want anyone to go too far into the river, and Diego helped with that, but mostly he just yelled and heaved in rocks so that they would make a big splash, and pretended to be a river monster, making the kids yell and laugh. He didn't think about chores or prison or debts or justice. He only thought about being the very best river monster he could be. He pretended that his throat hurt from yelling instead of from tear gas.

They played until the children got tired. Then they just sat on the rocks and watched the river flow by. Sister Rosa taught them all a little-kid song about animals. Diego sang along as though he wasn't a serious working man, but just a regular twelve-year-old kid.

Then he looked up at the bridge. It was a long way up, just like the bridge Mando had fallen from. This one was made of cement and steel. The one Mando had fallen from was made of ropes and planks, but they were both high, and the ground below both of them was harsh with rocks.

How scared he must have been, Diego thought. How hard he must have landed.

"You're not singing," Martino said. "You're crying."

Diego wiped his eyes and tried to bring himself under control, but a loud sob escaped from his throat.

Martino climbed into his lap.

They sat like that for a little while. Then Martino said he was hungry. Diego helped Sister Rosa gather the kids together and hike them up the hill – first to the bridge, then farther up to the safer place.

Shortly before sunset, the captain's voice came over the loudspeaker.

"I have some news for all of you. My superior officer has arrived. I now introduce you to Major Garcia."

The loudspeaker crackled as the microphone was passed from man to man. Then a new voice came on.

"This bridge will be cleared at sunrise tomorrow. You have my word as an officer and a Bolivian that nothing will happen before then, as long as my soldiers are not attacked first. My men, and my tanks, will stay behind the barricades. You are all free to disperse at any time tonight. You will not be stopped. You will not be arrested. But when the sun comes up, we *will* take back this bridge."

There was the rumbling of motors again. The tanks and trucks shifted to one side, and a giant bulldozer rolled down the middle of the highway. It stopped in front of the northern barrier and turned off its motor.

"Well, that's that," Diego said to Bonita, who was standing nearby. "It had to end some time." He was grateful it was over. It was beginning to look more and more like there was nothing in it for him, no matter what happened to the blockade. Maybe there would be more justice for the cocaleros down the line, but that wouldn't put any money in his pockets today.

"You see anybody leaving?" Bonita asked. "Do you see anybody packing up?"

"You mean people will stay? Knowing what's coming?"

"This is for our lives," Bonita said. "*Our* lives, not yours. Go if you want to."

Then she looked at him without the usual scorn on her face.

"You have family to get back to. My family is here. It will be all right if you go."

"What will happen in the morning?" he asked her. "What will the army do?"

"I don't know," she said. "But Emilio would. He went through this during the water protests. Let's ask him."

They looked for Emilio all over the bridge, and then they went up the hill to the ridge. He wasn't there either.

Diego went to an old woman by the fire.

"Have you seen Emilio? Vargas's son?"

"Vargas's son?" a woman replied, poking a stick into the fire. "A good boy. Polite. Went off with those older boys. The not-polite ones."

"You mean Dario and Leon?" Diego leaned over and yelled in the old woman's face. "You mean Dario and Leon! Why didn't you stop them?"

"What are you doing?" Bonita pulled him away and apologized to the old woman.

"We have to find them," Diego said, his panic rising. "They're up to something, and they've dragged Emilio into it. He'll get himself shot."

"Emilio's not that stupid," Bonita said.

"He wants his father to be proud of him."

"What?"

Diego didn't understand it either.

"When did they leave?" he demanded of the old woman. "Where did they go?"

"I've got my own work to attend to," she said. "I can't keep track of boys coming and going." She waved her fire-poking stick at Diego.

Bonita knelt down and spoke gently to the old woman in Quechua. The woman answered back, stroking Bonita on the cheek.

"You're a good girl," the woman said. "You know how to be respectful."

Bonita grabbed Diego's arm. "This way."

They ran the length of the open ridge, dodging around groups of parents trying to settle their children down for the night.

"Shouldn't we get Vargas?" Diego asked as he ran.

"There isn't time," Bonita told him. "Can't you run faster?"

The ridge ended with the forest. "There must be a trail," Bonita said. "Help me find it."

Night had fallen, and there was no moon. They skirted the edge of the woods trying to find the entrance until Bonita got fed up and plunged right into the trees.

"Wait!" Diego called. "Let's stick together!" There was nothing to be gained by getting lost.

By accident, they stumbled upon the trail that led south above the highway. In a short while they found themselves peering down through the trees at the convoy of military trucks and bulldozers. Soldiers were talking and laughing, eating their evening meal and listening to music on a radio.

"They must be down there somewhere," Diego said. "Leon was talking about sneaking around and attacking."

"You knew about this?" Bonita whispered, swatting him on the arm. "Why didn't you tell someone?"

"I thought it was just talk."

"Congratulations. You may have just gotten another friend killed."

"That's not going to happen!" Diego pushed past Bonita with such determination that she fell over. He heard her get up and follow him, but he didn't wait. He had to find Emilio.

The hill was fairly steep, and there was almost no light to see where he was walking. His foot slid once, knocking debris down the bank. He and Bonita froze, terrified that the army would hear and start shooting, but the soldiers were too busy eating and talking to notice.

Now crawling on his behind, Diego inched closer and closer to the camp. He kept his eyes wide open, straining to see Emilio and the others in the dark.

It was Leon who gave them away. He was arguing with Dario.

"I made the thing! I should be the one to throw it!"

"We both made it," Dario said. "Who got the gasoline?"

"Who got the bottles?"

"Who *broke* one of the bottles?" Dario hissed in return. "We stick to the plan. Emilio, take this one, crawl under the bulldozer, light it, then crawl out like mad before it goes off. As soon as the bulldozer explodes, I'll throw this one."

Bonita was right beside Diego. She pointed at

172   *Deborah Ellis*

the shadow that was Emilio, starting to creep down the hill.

"Go and get him," she told Diego. "I'll stop the others." Then she was gone.

A dance song that one of the soldiers liked came on the radio, and he turned up the volume. Diego used the music to cover up the sound of him sliding down the rest of the hill, getting there at the same time as Emilio. He tackled Emilio to the ground just as Dario and Leon let out a yell. Bonita must have scared them.

The soldiers sprang into action. Diego rolled with Emilio under a military truck, out of sight. He grabbed the gasoline-filled bottle and rolled it away down the pavement.

A spotlight was shone on the hill. Soldiers rushed up to grab Dario and Leon. Diego watched them being brought down the hill, Dario still holding on to his bottle of gasoline.

Boot-clad feet moved quickly all around the truck. Shouting went back and forth as soldiers radioed to the major at the north end of the bridge. Diego waited in fear for the soldiers to bring Bonita off the hill, but it didn't happen. She had gotten away.

It was time to get out of there. Diego stuck his head out from beneath the truck and checked to make sure it was safe to leave. He held out his hand to Emilio. In a flash, they were back under the cover of the trees.

"You ruined our plan!" Emilio swung at Diego. "You ruined everything!"

Diego ducked and raised his arms against Emilio's blows.

Bonita appeared behind them and pulled Emilio away.

"You're an idiot," she told him. "We'd better get back."

The major was on the loudspeaker again. His voice reached them just as they cleared the woods and arrived back on the ridge.

"Two of your people have been arrested carrying a Molotov cocktail they were intending to use against the army," he said. "If there is one more incident like this, we will clear the bridge before dawn, and without any warning."

Suddenly Vargas was in front of them. He wrapped his son in a big hug.

"Someone told me you'd gone off with those men," Vargas said. "I was so afraid! You must never do anything like that again!" He looked over at Diego and Bonita. "Thank you," he said to them, then walked away with Emilio to sit with him by the fire.

"That was close," Bonita said, heading back down to the bridge.

Diego kept his eyes on Vargas and Emilio together by the fire. He saw Vargas speak softly to his son, smooth his hair and kiss the top of his head. When Emilio looked away, Diego saw Vargas wipe tears from his eyes.

Emilio's father loved him. He loved him even if he was sick a lot.

He loved him even when he made stupid mistakes.

CHAPTER SIXTEEN

It was not a night for sleeping, although some people did, and some people tried to.

"We'll need our rest for tomorrow," they said.

"Tomorrow could be the end," others said. "We can sleep when we're dead."

The temperature had dropped. Mrs. Ricardo gave Diego an extra poncho and ordered him to put it on. It smelled of tear gas and donkey, but it felt like a warm hug.

Diego was too tired to sleep. He went looking for Bonita.

She was sitting on the bridge, her back against the railing, not far from where the guitar player and the zampona players were playing their sweet, sad nighttime music. She didn't object when he sat down beside her.

"Some people have left," she said. "They've gone back to their farms. Others will leave in the morning."

"You can't really blame them," Diego said. "It's not as if staying is going to solve their problems. Your neighbor's kids still won't have any shoes, no matter what happens in the morning."

"You should go, then," she said.

"Yes," Diego agreed. "I should." But he didn't move.

"Your family depends on you," he said. "You're the oldest. You have responsibilities. Maybe you should think about leaving before the morning comes."

"You're right," she said, without a whisper of argument in her voice. "If either of my parents dies, the other would be lost without me. If my father dies, I can take over his work on the farm. If my mother dies, I can look after Martino and Santo. Things happen. They could die. Tomorrow, later. Things happen."

Their shoulders were touching. "But I'm staying," she went on. "I'm staying because it would be easy to leave. I'm staying because it will always be easy to leave, and if I leave now, it will get harder and harder to stay. I'd spend my whole life leaving."

Diego was going to say that just because you make a decision once doesn't mean you'll make the same decision all the time, but he didn't. Besides, he knew what she meant. He knew of adults in both his parents' prisons who made the decision to stop looking after themselves – to stop washing, stop thinking, stop caring – and that became a hard habit to break.

"Are you staying?" Bonita asked him.

It was time to ask himself that question. Maybe he could get some kind of work in the village north of the blockade, earn a few bolivianos, then hitch rides home with money in his pocket. That was the reason he left Cochabamba in the first place. Getting gassed and shot at was not part of the plan. There was nothing, really, keeping him here. In fact, it would be smarter to go.

But he would have to tell his parents that he'd walked away. They'd tell him it was the right thing to do, that his safety came before anything else. They'd mean it, too, because they were his

Deborah Ellis

parents. But there would be something in their eyes – not disappointment, but not pride, either.

"I'm going to stay," he said.

Bonita didn't say anything for such a long time, he thought she'd fallen asleep. Then she asked, "Are you afraid?"

"Yes."

"So am I." She took hold of his hand and they sat that way, listening to the night music and waiting for the dawn.

CHAPTER SEVENTEEN

✳

Morning rose with a heavy mist off the river, engulfing the bridge in a gray, slow-swirling cloud.

"Diego," someone called from the north barricade. "Someone to see you over here."

Diego came out of his doze. Bonita was already up and away. He rubbed his eyes and got to his feet.

All across the bridge, people were slowly stirring. Diego made his way to the north barricade through the half-light of morning. When he got there, the captain was waiting for him.

"Are you all right?" the captain asked.

Diego didn't answer. This was the man who was going to shoot at his friends the very first day of the blockade.

"I've been ordered back to Cochabamba," the captain said. "I'm leaving this morning. Now, in fact. You can come with me."

Diego was too shocked to respond right away. He looked back at the people on the bridge.

"I can't…"

"Diego, it's going to get bad. This major isn't going to count off and bluff. He's *going* to clear the bridge! What good would it do…"

"You mean you weren't going to order us to be shot?"

"Of course not."

Diego believed him, and was glad. He thought about the captain's offer. Then he thought about Bonita, and the rest of the Ricardos, and Vargas and Emilio. They were all staying. They had no one to give them a lift to a safer place.

"I can't leave," Diego said.

"Take care of yourself. If I ever have a son, I hope he turns out to be just like you." He shook Diego's hand and turned to go.

"Captain?" Diego called out. "Which way is Cochabamba?"

The captain pointed up the hill behind him.

"Just follow the highway," he said. Then, with a wave, he was gone.

Diego returned to the blockade. The cocaleros were gathering for a final meeting before the sun came up.

"My friends," said Vargas, his voice bringing them all together. "Comrades. Campesinos. I have something to say to you."

Vargas spoke without a microphone, his arm around Emilio's shoulder. His words became trapped in the fog and hovered over them. Diego joined the others, gathering in close to be able to hear.

"It's not that long ago that, before people like us could meet with a Bolivian official, they would spray us with DDT, because they were afraid we would spread lice and germs. Today we are able to shut down the country. One day we will govern the country, and even those who look down on us will be forced to meet with us as equals.

"We are here today with nothing but our bodies and our courage. We have come together, and we have acted, and we have shown the world that we are strong."

All over the bridge, Diego heard people say, "We are!" and "Solidarity!" but they didn't say these things loudly. The moment was too solemn.

"We are engaged in a very old struggle, the struggle of poor people to control the land they work and sweat over, to control their resources, and to control their lives. It is the struggle of the Hebrew slaves in Egypt. It is the struggle of the people of South Africa to end apartheid. It is the struggle of every working person in history to liberate themselves from the rich people who exploit them."

Vargas moved about the little circle the protesters had made for him. When he talked, he looked right into people's faces.

"Cocaleros, none of us is rich. We struggle to feed our families, we struggle to send our children to school. Our lives may never be comfortable. But when we go to our graves, with our last breath and thoughts we will know we lived in dignity and stood by those who needed us.

"The struggle of the moment will be played out here, and soon, but it will not be our last struggle. It does not matter what they do to us today. We cannot be frightened. We cannot be silenced. And we cannot be stopped."

The words of victory from the crowd got a little louder as people found their courage. They bumped up against each other, gaining strength from one another. Diego stood with the Ricardos, their arms around each other as they stood side by side and shoulder to shoulder with the others on the bridge.

Diego felt tall standing together with the other cocaleros. They were all tired. They were all hungry. Many, like Diego, still had eyes and throats that burned from the tear gas. Diego knew something was going to happen, very serious and very soon. He was afraid – and yet, he wasn't. In this moment, in spite of everything, Diego was happy.

The group broke apart. The sun would soon be up. Diego helped pick up blankets and other debris from the bridge. It wouldn't do for protesters to trip on things while they were running. He could feel the tension in the people around him. He saw it on their faces – a calm, hard, scared determination. He wondered if they were asking themselves the same questions he was

184   *Deborah Ellis*

asking himself. Would he be brave? Would he be proud of himself at the end of the day? Would he stand by his brothers and sisters?

He thought he would, but he wouldn't know for sure until it was all over.

Diego carried an armload of blankets up to the ridge where the little children and their care-givers were staying. The blankets would be good for the wounded who would be brought up to the ridge to be taken care of. Sister Rosa was there helping to set up the first-aid station.

Diego knelt down beside her and helped spread out the blankets.

"You should leave," he said. "You and the other nuns. The sun will be up soon."

Sister Rosa flashed her bright, wide smile and gently pushed the hair out of Diego's eyes.

"We are exactly where we need to be," she said. She didn't seem scared at all. Diego smiled back at her. Smiling made him feel braver.

He returned to the bridge.

The army had moved up the road from the south end and were now just a short distance beyond the south barrier. Diego smelled diesel fuel again. This time he was better prepared for tear gas. His kerchief was freshly wet with vinegar and tied firmly around his neck, ready to pull up over his nose and mouth when the gas started flying.

He took up a position behind the south barrier. He could see the soldiers getting ready for the order to take the bridge.

Behind him he could hear the cocaleros reassuring themselves that everything would be all right. They were planning to lie down on the road in front of the army. Diego couldn't bear to think what would happen if the army kept rolling right over them.

"The mothers are doing a blockade of babies," Bonita said, as Mrs. Ricardo and other mothers walked out to the bare part of the highway between the army and the south barrier. They each had a baby in their arms or strapped to their backs in an aguayo. They sat proudly, bowler hats perched tall on their heads, and nursed or sang to their babies, steps away from the army.

"What are they doing?" Diego asked.

"Shaming the army into stopping," Mr. Ricardo said, and added, almost to himself, "I hope."

"Where's Martino?"

"Up on the ridge rolling bandages. We can't keep track of him down here."

The sky over the river began to brighten. The sun was coming up.

"This is your last warning," the major's voice boomed out over the loudspeaker. "This is absolutely your last chance to leave. We are taking back this bridge."

Then the sun rose up, quite definitely. The morning had broken. Diego heard the revving of motors, saw the soldiers clamp on their gas masks and point their rifles. He pulled his kerchief up over his nose and mouth and watched the troops begin to advance.

The bulldozer came closer and closer to the line of women and children stretched across the highway. Diego could hear some of the babies crying and their mothers singing. He grabbed on to Mr. Ricardo's and Bonita's hands, squeezing them in fear as the blade of the bulldozer shovel came closer and closer to Mrs. Ricardo, Santo and the others.

Then it stopped.

Diego saw the television camera at the side of the road, filming everything.

From behind the bulldozer came streams of soldiers, a hundred of them, maybe more, faceless in gas masks. Working in teams, they lifted each mother and child off the road and carried them back behind army lines. The women didn't fight, but they certainly didn't help, either. The soldiers had to do all the work.

Beside him, Diego felt Mr. Ricardo breathe a sigh of relief.

"They're just arresting them," he said. "They'll be all right."

It didn't take long for the soldiers to carry the women away, and the bulldozer started smashing through the south barrier. The first tear gas canisters landed on the bridge. People scrambled to toss them back. Diego's eyes began to sting.

He couldn't tell for sure what was happening at the north end, but he guessed it was more of the same. The roar of machines was behind him as well as ahead of him, and then the helicopter appeared. The propellers blew away some of the gas.

The bulldozer easily pushed through the barricade Diego and the others had worked so hard to build. As the army advanced, the cocaleros retreated to the middle of the bridge. More tear gas came flying in. A canister landed near Diego. He picked it up and threw it back, then felt a terrible pain in his chest. The blow knocked him to the ground.

He heard rifle shots and saw others fall near him.

Was he shot? His chest hurt so much.

"Everyone lie down," Vargas called out. Diego looked up to see the television camera in his face. All around him people lay down on the bridge until the army could not move one more step without running over somebody.

Diego felt himself being lifted and carried off the bridge by a soldier in a gas mask.

It was over. The blockade was over.

CHAPTER EIGHTEEN

"Where does it hurt?" he heard Sister Rosa ask.

He opened his eyes. She was leaning over him.

"Is it your chest? Let me see."

The army had turned one lane of the highway into a holding pen for the demonstrators, using portable fencing and rolls of barbed wire. All the cocaleros from the bridge were being held there.

At first the soldiers wouldn't let the nuns in to provide medical care.

"Go back to your church," they said. Then two of the nuns – Sister Rosa and Sister Juanita – sat down in front of the soldiers and refused to move, until they were finally carried away and put in the pen, too. The third nun, Sister Maria, was up on the ridge looking after the children and the wounded who hadn't been arrested.

"They were shooting rubber bullets," Sister Rosa said, feeling Diego's chest for broken ribs. "You might have cracked something. I'll bind you up just in case, but you should get checked out by a doctor as soon as you can."

Diego didn't know when that might be. The bandages around his chest made him feel a little better.

"You'll have a big bruise," Sister Rosa said as she helped him put his shirt back on, "but I think you'll be all right."

The protesters were packed in pretty tightly. Diego leaned against someone who leaned against him in return. At last there was nothing to do. At last he could rest.

In just a short time the army and its bulldozers managed to wipe out all traces of the community on the bridge. Boulders and branches, tarps and old tires were all shoved away into the trees and down the river bank. Before very long, cars started rolling across the bridge again.

"Is everyone all right?" Vargas asked, making

his way through the crowd in the pen. There were a lot of wounded, mostly from flying gas canisters and rubber bullets. Some people had tripped when they were trying to get out of the way of the army, and they had scrapes and sprains.

When Vargas saw Diego, he said, "I want to thank you again for stopping my son. He could have been killed. I don't understand why he would try to do such a foolish thing."

"Tell him you're proud of him," Diego said, with his eyes closed. For some reason his chest didn't hurt so much when his eyes were closed.

"He knows I'm proud of him," Vargas said.

"Remind him," said Diego. He felt Vargas's hand on his head. Then the union leader walked away.

Families found each other and sat together. The Ricardos found Diego. They sat and dozed and watched the cars and trucks and buses go by. Diego slept. Every now and then he woke with a jolt, sure he was supposed to be doing something, but there was nothing to do.

In the middle of the day, the major came to the fence and asked to speak to Vargas. The two

Deborah Ellis

men talked for awhile. Then Vargas called a meeting.

"The major is prepared to release us if we promise not to reblockade the highway."

"For how long must we hold this promise?" someone asked.

"He did not say. All over Bolivia, traffic is moving again. The blockades have all been lifted, but that does not mean people have given up. Some are marching to La Paz. Some are getting back their strength so they can be ready the next time they are called. It is a decision that affects us all. If we agree to it, we must keep our word. The government lies, but we don't have to."

People talked and argued and had their say, but the outcome was clear. There was a time to protest and a time to go back to their farms and try to build their lives again. The cocaleros vowed not to reblockade the road today. The major hadn't really asked for anything else.

They were let out of the pen a few at a time.

"Go back to your homes," they were ordered. "If you linger here, you will be arrested." People were tired. It was time to go home.

Finally, toward the end of the afternoon, the

Ricardos were allowed to leave, Diego with them.

"Diego," called Vargas from inside the pen. He had declared he would stay inside until everyone else had been released.

Diego went over to the fence. Vargas slipped a piece of paper through the opening.

"Here is the address of the union headquarters in Cochabamba. We could use a good runner like you to run errands for us. For pay," he said. "And after school."

Diego thanked him and shook his hand as best as he could through the wires.

"Tell Emilio goodbye for me," he said.

"You'll see him soon," said Vargas. "He'll stop being mad. You two will become good, good friends."

Diego rejoined the Ricardos.

"Come back to the farm with us," Mr. Ricardo urged him. "Rest there for awhile."

"And work," said Bonita.

"I'm going home," Diego said. There were cars and trucks rolling on the highway now. One of them might give him a ride.

They didn't say goodbye. He just hugged

them – even Bonita – and headed to the bridge.

Soldiers were directing the one lane of traffic that was open. Diego walked through them and crossed the bridge one last time. When he got to the north end, he looked back once, then kept going. His family was waiting.

He would walk to the village and try to get a ride, even part way. He'd get as far as he could before dark, then start again in the morning. He wasn't afraid to sleep outside by himself. At the moment, he wasn't afraid of anything.

He kept walking and could soon see the top of the little village church peeking out through the trees. He thought about the bald priest going without his lunch, and he laughed.

He had just rounded the bend when he saw a man sitting on the hood of a jeep, leaning against the windshield.

It was the captain.

"I'd almost given up," the captain said.

"Are you waiting for me?"

"Unless you want to walk back to Cochabamba. Are you all right?"

Diego felt the bandage on his chest.

"Yes," he said. "I'm all right." He climbed into

the jeep. There was food and water in the back seat. The captain started the engine, and they were soon moving down the highway.

* * *

The sun was up and Cochabamba was awake by the time the captain steered the jeep into San Sebastian Square.

It was all as Diego remembered it. The park in the center with the gardens and fountains, the stray dogs sleeping in the sun, the Aymara woman selling biscuits and candies from the sidewalk stand, the ugly stone women's prison and the ugly stone men's prison, with the furniture and dog houses the prisoners made stacked out front.

"I'll come around in a few days," the captain said. "Do you want me to go in with you?"

Diego shook his head.

"They'll be glad to see you," the captain said. "They'll be overjoyed."

And then Diego was alone in the square, at the corner across from the two prisons. Behind the walls of one was his mother, who would hug him and kiss him and cry.

But first he would go to see his father. And Mando's.

Diego took a deep breath, crossed the street, and went through the doors of the men's prison.

CHAPTER NINETEEN

Diego lay in the sun on the grass of the Plaza Colón, on the edge of a group of glue-sniffing boys who lived on the streets. This was his third day in the park, and he was beginning to wonder if the plan would work.

Across the footpath, sitting on a park bench by the fountain and pretending to read a newspaper sat the captain. He wore dark glasses and day-off-work clothes. Every now and then he would get up and go for a stroll, or switch benches, or put on a cap to try to change his appearance a bit.

Diego's part was easier. All he had to do was lie on the grass and look stupid.

Diego's parents had taken some convincing

to give their permission. Diego had been back for a week, and he had spent most of that time inside the prisons with his family. Now that he was back, his parents didn't want to let him out of their sight again.

But the captain went to see them and promised to look out for Diego every single minute. They finally relented when Diego told them it was his way to do something about Mando's death.

The captain was working on getting Diego's parents out of prison.

"It won't happen overnight," he told Diego. "The legal system hates to admit it made a mistake. But I won't give up."

Diego knew that the captain would have a lot more power if he could break up a drug ring. So they spent their days in the park, the captain keeping watch on Diego, and Diego keeping watch for someone looking to hire street boys to work in the pits where coca leaves were turned into the paste that would be made into cocaine.

Keeping watch over both of them were a few plainclothes officers under the captain's command, ready to move in when they got the signal.

The square was getting crowded with people

coming out of shops and offices to take their lunch breaks under the trees. Ice-cream and orange-juice sellers were busy, and the bells were ringing in the cathedral to call people in to mid-day mass.

Diego was close to drifting off in the hot sun when he thought he saw someone he recognized. He wanted to jump up and look closer, but he forced himself to keep still and keep watching.

With a small nod of his head, he signaled to the captain to follow his gaze. A small nod told him the captain understood. They both waited until the man got closer, heading straight for the glue-sniffing boys and for Diego.

Diego tucked his face into the crook of his arm so it would be hidden except for his eyes.

Maybe, for once, something would be easy. Maybe, for once, something would work.

The man was who was walking through the square was Rock, the thug who had taken Diego and Mando into the coca pits.

And he was heading straight into their trap.

Diego allowed himself a small smile.

"For you, Mando," he whispered. Then he got ready to enjoy himself.

Justice was about to happen in Cochabamba.

⁎

"People lost their fear of bullets; they lost their fear of repression. The ghosts of past times of terror were defeated on the blockades." — Oscar Olivera, organizer of the water protests in Cochabamba, Bolivia, 2000

(Quoted in *¡Cochabamba! Water War in Bolivia* by Oscar Olivera and Tom Lewis, South End Press, 2004)

AUTHOR'S NOTE

Coca is a sacred plant to the indigenous people of Bolivia – one of the poorest countries in the Western hemisphere. The native people chew the leaves and make them into a tea to ease living and working at high altitudes. But coca can also be mixed with chemicals and turned into a paste that can be made into cocaine, a drug that is smuggled into North America and sold illegally. If North Americans and others did not buy cocaine in large quantities, this drug trade would not exist.

During the past three decades, with the backing of the United States, the Bolivian government has used special police units to destroy the country's coca crops, bringing economic hard-

ship to the already poor cocaleros (coca growers). The cocaleros organized themselves into a
union and, in the fall of 2000, Bolivia was shut
down by massive protests by cocaleros, farmers
and other workers such as teachers. More than
ten thousand cocaleros blockaded highways all
over the country, stopping traffic and bringing
the day-to-day functioning of the country to a
standstill. Both protesters and police were killed
in the clashes, and many were injured.

As a result of negotiations to end the road
blocks, cocaleros were allowed a voice on the
committee that made decisions about programs
to encourage alternative crops to coca, but coca
crop eradication continued.

Road blockades continued, off and on, over
the next few years, as the Bolivian people tried
to claim some control over their country's vast
natural resources, such as oil and natural gas.
In 2005, the people elected Evo Morales, the
former head of the coca growers' union, as
their president. He ran on promises to regain
control of those resources, to rewrite the constitution to ensure greater rights for indigenous
Bolivians, and to legalize the growing of coca.

Bolivia now has a new constitution, and work is underway to find new, legal uses and markets for the sacred coca leaf.

GLOSSARY

Aguayo – A large square piece of cloth used to carry things on a person's back.

Anu – A root vegetable grown in Bolivia.

Aymara – A group of indigenous people who live in the Andean region of South America, mainly in Bolivia. Also the traditional language of the Aymara.

Boliviano – Bolivian money.

Campesino – A farmer; peasant; working person.

Centavo – Bolivian money; there are one hundred centavos in a boliviano.

Chagas – A disease spread by the vinchuca beetle, which often lives in clay walls and thatched roofs. It kills thousands of people each year in South America and makes millions more ill.

Charango – A small guitar.

Chicha – Corn beer, sometimes also made from sweet potatoes.

Chicheria – A place that makes and sells chicha.

Chupe – A thick soup containing grains, vegetables and meat.

Coca – A small shrub grown in the Andes. Its leaves have been used by the indigenous people of the Andes for centuries for food, medicine and religious rituals.

Cocaine – An illegal drug made from coca leaves that have been processed into a paste.

Cocalero – A coca farmer.

Empanada – A pastry filled with meat or cheese.

Gringo – Slang for a citizen of the United States.

Holy Week – The time around Good Friday and Easter in the Christian calendar.

Pollera skirts – Short skirts with many layers.

Quechua – Language spoken by people who live in certain parts of the Andean region, including Bolivia. People who speak Quechua are often called Quechua.

Rubber bullets – Bullets encased in rubber, used for crowd control.

Tostada – A non-alcoholic drink made from barley, honey and cinnamon.

Zampona – A flute made of reeds.

DEBORAH ELLIS has achieved international acclaim with her courageous, sensitive and dramatic books that give Western readers a glimpse into the plight of children in developing countries. She has won the Governor General's Award, Sweden's Peter Pan Prize, the Ruth Schwartz Award, the University of California's Middle East Book Award, the Jane Addams Children's Book Award and the Vicky Metcalf Award. A long-time feminist and anti-war activist, she is perhaps best known for the Breadwinner trilogy, which has been published around the world in seventeen languages, with more than half a million dollars of royalties donated to Street Kids International and to Women for Women, an organization that supports education projects for Afghan girls in refugee camps in Pakistan. Deb lives in Simcoe, Ontario.